Sidestep

Sidestep

Sharon Henegar

Saturday Books

Published by Saturday Books
3160 Holiday Dr. S.
Salem, OR 97302

ISBN 978-0-9961980-1-1
Henegar, Sharon L.
Sidestep / Sharon L. Henegar
Identity Theft—Fiction
Ecology—Fiction
Salem, Oregon—Fiction
Mystery Fiction

Dedicated to
Karen Kruger.
She made me do it!

Sidestep

1

I only meant to step out of my life for a few days. It never occurred to me that my life would be gone when I tried to step back in.

The first hint came at breakfast. I drove down to Hood River from the little cabin on the mountain where I had spent the past week. Yesterday had been blustery, cold and wet, so when dawn brought clear skies and that golden autumn sunlight that turns the world into a hazy dream, I had to put the top down on my car and take a drive.

My dog Clover was strapped into her seatbelt in the back seat. She's as tough as an old boot from all the running and retrieving she does, but at thirty pounds she would never survive a deployed airbag if I let her sit shotgun.

We stuck to backroads going down the mountain, though a short stretch on Interstate 84 was unavoidable. I rolled up all the windows to minimize the wind and kept to the right lane so I could go slower than the rest of the juggernauts speeding toward Portland. When we reached Hood River my short hair was standing on end. I batted it down, raked my fingers through it, and glanced back at Clover.

She wore the happy grin of a dog who has just had her nostrils filled with supercharged air and her ears whipped around in a frenzy. Our eyes met for a moment.

"You're welcome," I told her.

I found the breakfast café I'd Yelped on the main drag. Half a block further a car was just leaving a parking place, a nice long one that I could nose into instead of having to actually parallel park—not my best driving skill. I glanced around the interior of the car and decided I'd better put the lid back up. There were a few things I'd be sorry to have stolen, items I'd brought along on our journey from North Carolina that I didn't trust the movers to ship safely to the new place. A push of a button later the car was as secure as a ragtop gets. I grabbed Clover's leash from the seat beside me, freed her from the back seat, and led her down the street.

One small table was unoccupied on the café patio, back in a shaded corner. I sat down and dropped Clover's leash. She sniffed the area around my chair then settled at my feet, front paws crossed. Her amber eyes inspected the scene around us, and I saw her nostrils quivering as she read the secrets brought to her on the morning breeze.

"Coffee?" My waiter was of medium height and muscular, with tanned skin and ruddy cheeks. I could easily imagine him whipping his way across the Columbia with the other windsurfers. He laid a laminated menu on the table, then set down a glass of ice water.

"Hot tea," I replied. "Something black, but not Earl Grey."

"Darjeeling?"

I nodded. "And some cream, please."

He returned in about five minutes with the tea, but not the cream. "Do you know what you'd like to order?"

I handed him the menu. "A short stack of the cinnamon French toast, two eggs scrambled, and the cream for my tea."

"Oops, sorry about that." He tucked the menu under his order pad and scribbled, then looked around at the other tables. Two ladies were gathering up their purses. "Hey Janice, are you done with that cream pitcher?"

"Sure am." She rose, picked up the creamer, and held it out to him. As he took it she looked at me and said, "There's plenty left. Gina always thinks she wants cream and then never uses any."

"Thanks," I grinned back at her. I heard Clover's whippy tail thumping against my chair leg.

"That's a handsome dog. Looks like she knows a thing or two."

"Oh, she knows everything." I looked down into Clover's bright eyes. "And then some."

Janice chuckled and turned away with a little wave. My waiter set down the creamer near my teacup. "Back in a few minutes with your food."

The café got extra points when I saw I'd been given loose tea steeping in a china pot. A handsome pewter strainer sat on the cup. When I poured out the first cup, my nostrils filled with that lovely tea aroma and I gave a deep sigh. Maybe this was a good omen, and I'd been right to turn my life in an entirely new direction.

I took a sip, then reached for my purse and took out my Kindle Fire. I'd finished the book I was reading last night and needed to find a new one to try. I settled on one called *Sleeping Dogs Lie*; it sounded fun, and some of the characters were dogs. "Maybe you'll like it too, you can read it when I'm done," I told Clover. I clicked the Buy It Now button.

The next screen asked for a password.

I frowned. It never asked me for a password at this point. I had set things up with a password to get into the device, but once I was in, this particular password had been memorized.

Until today.

And I had no idea what the password was.

For a moment I regretted my decision not to use one of those online password sites. I'd opted instead to keep my own list, in a randomly named document on

4

my laptop. I have a good memory for lots of things, but there were so many passwords to keep up with these days. Every card in your wallet had a different one, not to mention every website you interacted with, from your bank to the site where you found your knitting patterns. Like most people, I'd started out years ago using the same code for just about everything. But by now I had seen too many warnings about the necessity for unique—and frequently changed—passwords. So I had a zillion passwords and could only remember about three of them.

I just wouldn't be reading a new book through breakfast. No big deal. When I got back to the cabin I'd find my password list, buy the e-book, and be back in business.

I poured more tea and sat back, enjoying the sunshine. I inspected the other breakfasters, a varied lot. People in business suits, people in every variety of casual clothing. One large table was surrounded by a group of eight teenage girls. I caught talk about dorm rooms and class schedules. Perhaps they were high school friends getting together for the last time before heading to college.

Breakfast actually lived up to the hype I'd read about the place. My sister and I had "collected" French toast through our childhood, always ordering that when we were taken out to breakfast. We had taken our French Toast Rating System quite seriously. Feeling very Gallic, we had used up to five Eiffel Towers to denote the quality of the food. Of course, a really cute waiter could influence us to give more

Eiffel Towers to a less than stellar product. I still ordered it in her memory, sending her a little mental report on how it compared.

Clover was happy as well. Our waiter brought her a heavy china bowl of water and a little plate of homemade dog biscuits. "Our dessert baker invented these for her pets," he explained, "and now every dog in town expects them when they come here."

He checked on my progress two or three times, refilling the teapot with steaming hot water without being asked. When he presented the bill he said, "No hurry, just whenever."

I fished out a credit card and laid it on top of the bill on the little tray. "Here you go." I poured out more tea into my cup, and thought about how Clover and I might spend the day.

My waiter was back at my side, proffering my credit card. "I'm sorry," he said quietly, "but this card wouldn't run. Do you have another we could use?"

"What? Are you kidding?" I shook my head and thought for a moment. "I used it a couple of days ago for gas. I wonder if they messed up the strip or something."

"Could be." He looked at me expectantly. I grabbed my purse and pulled out my billfold. "Here, this should work." I handed him the other credit card I had with me, one that I rarely use. The account had a high line of credit and I knew I hadn't charged anything on it for months.

But soon he was back again, his voice even lower. "Umm, we tried several times and the machine didn't like this one either." He handed me the card.

"Gosh," I said lightly, hoping that the uneasiness fluttering among the French toast didn't show, "I wonder what's going on. Sorry about that. Let me just give you the cash. How much was it?"

Breakfast paid for, I gathered up my purse and Clover's leash. I had planned to take a walk around Hood River, maybe go for a drive around the surrounding orchards and admire all the apples and pears waiting to be picked. But the password and credit card snafus made me decidedly uneasy. I hurried back to the car and strapped Clover into her seatbelt. The bright sunshine seemed dimmed, and the air felt like storm clouds were hiding just over the horizon.

2

The clock on my car's dashboard read 3:11. I pulled into the parking lot of the apartment complex I had chosen for my first few months in Salem. Unlocking my seatbelt, I reached back to give Clover a pat. "Okay, baby girl, we're here. I'll go in and get the key, we'll find the apartment, and then we'll figure out what the hell is going on."

I'd rented the little cabin on Mount Hood for eight days, wanting a laid-back oasis before diving into the eddies of a new job. The long drive across the country had felt like a voyage of years. Indifferent road food left me feeling stale and bloated. I rather envied my dog her unvarying diet of dry kibble.

We had both settled into the cabin with sighs of relief. We spent the days taking long walks, Clover following her eager nose and giving chase to a wide variety of birds. Her one encounter with a skunk ended without incident, as she recognized the panic in my voice and immediately (and surprisingly) came bounding back to me. She got a big jackpot of treats for that.

A herd of wild turkeys ended up chasing her and after that she gave them all the space they wanted.

After returning from my breakfast in town, I fired up my laptop and found my passwords document. I tried again to buy *Sleeping Dogs Lie*. My password didn't work. I tried a couple of variants, thinking perhaps I had updated it and not changed the file. No dice. I glanced at the list and noticed the password for the knitting site. That one didn't work either.

I went to the top of the list and started working my way down, skipping any financial sites since I was on someone else's Wi-Fi account.

None of them worked.

Even the most innocuous of websites would not let me in. From Amazon to Craigslist to Twitter and YouTube, I was shut out. Even goddam Martha Stewart had locked the door.

What the hell had happened?

We had the cabin for another day, but I couldn't stay any longer. There was no more peace to be found on the mountain. I had to know what was going on as soon as I could. I loaded the car, set my GPS, Gladys, on the "fastest route" setting, and we barreled back downhill to the freeway. I kept my focus resolutely on driving, skirting Portland and picking up Interstate 5. Gladys eventually took me off the freeway onto Salem Parkway and past the downtown area. I realized as I passed the library that I had no memory of the trip whatsoever.

Now, parked outside the hollow core door labeled "Manager" at my new apartment complex, I took a deep breath, rubbed Clover's soft ear one more time for luck, grabbed my purse and climbed out of the car. Knocked on the door. Waited. Noticed a doorbell and pressed it. Waited.

Knocked again.

A window opened in the apartment directly over the manager's door, and a head emerged. Wild blue hair hung down and obscured the features of the face, but nothing could have dimmed the volume of that voice.

"Yeah? Waddaya want? It's not office hours. They don't pay me enough to be on call twenty four seven."

"Oh, sorry, I didn't know you had limited hours. I just need to pick up the key for my apartment."

"What key? What apartment? I don't know what the hell you're talking about. Who the hell are you?"

I was getting a crick in my neck from staring straight up at her. I took a step back, rubbing my neck and trying a smile. "I'm Beth Harding." No response, just a glare. "Beth Harding," I repeated. "I've just moved here from North Carolina. The movers should have delivered my stuff a few days ago, and I arranged to pick up the key when I got here."

A hand reached out to sweep hair from her eyes, which were heavily made up and lined top and bottom with black. "Don't be ridiculous. Get out of here."

"What do you mean? I've paid for an apartment, I sent my belongings here on a moving van a week and a half ago, and I need my key." As an afterthought I added, "Please."

"Look, I don't know what you're trying to pull, but you can just forget it."

I felt as though I had stepped into quicksand and was being sucked under. "I'm not trying to 'pull' anything. I've had a long trip and I just want my key."

She dragged a long breath through her teeth in a hiss. "Well, for your information, Beth Harding arrived here on Tuesday *with* the moving van of her stuff. She told me she'd found another apartment closer to her job and canceled the lease on this one. She had to forfeit her deposit of course, but we have a waiting list and that apartment has been filled. And she and the moving van drove off. So like I said, lady, you're not Beth Harding, and you can go try your scam somewhere else."

"But—here, look." I reached into my purse and pulled out my billfold. "I have my driver's li—"

The blue hair withdrew and the window slammed shut. I stood with my mouth hanging open as a tidal wave of heat rushed up from my feet to my face. I stabbed the doorbell again, and pounded on the door for good measure. The window above slid open and a pitcher full of cold water dashed down on me from above.

"Get the hell out before I call the cops!" And the window banged shut again.

In a daze I turned back to the car, wiping water off my face. Once inside, door locked, I realized I was shaking with mingled rage and fear. I snapped the seatbelt on. "Hold on, Clover, we need to get out of here."

Turning right onto the street in front of the apartments, I drove for several blocks before I spotted a large parking lot by a grocery store. I pulled in and parked in the corner furthest from the door. Reaching back as far as I could I released Clover from her seatbelt, and in a nanosecond she was in my lap, licking my face. I hugged her hard.

"Clover, what is going on? The passwords, the apartment." She thumped her tail against the passenger seat and gave me another little smooch. A sudden thought assailed me. "Oh. My. God. What's going to happen when I show up for my new job on Monday?"

I tried to think but my mind was blank. "Okay. I—I don't have any idea what to do. What's a logical next step?"

Clover uttered a little woof.

"Okay. Right. Take care of the dog. You need food, water, shelter, and a place to potty. I can handle that. Let me put your leash on you and we'll take a little walk, then you can have a drink. Then we'll look for a place to spend the night, maybe the weekend."

A new thought jumped to the front of my mind. My credit card hadn't worked at breakfast, and given the scene at the apartment and the changing of all my passwords, it wasn't likely to have miraculously healed itself since then. I grabbed my purse from the passenger seat and pulled out my billfold. I had exactly $237.11 to my name. My debit card was unlikely to work any better than the credit card, but I'd better find out. I turned on the Kindle and found I was in a Wi-Fi zone. I sent a quick jot of gratitude to whatever lucky star had left me this one piece of technology that still worked.

Quickly I located the nearest ATM for my bank.

"Baby girl, hop in back. It's not very far. Let's see if we can get any more cash."

The drive into downtown Salem took me through a comfortable neighborhood with Victorian and Craftsman houses surrounding a large park. I crossed Mission Street, passed the public library, and followed Gladys the GPS's directions to my destination. There were a couple of empty parking spaces in front of the ATM. "Wait here," I told Clover, and hopped out.

Before I trusted my card to a machine, I decided to try a teller inside. But the door was securely locked, and I saw from the hours painted on the door that they had closed a few minutes ago. This bank still kept banker's hours. I returned to the ATM, pleased to see how steady my hands were as I inserted the debit card into the slot. I breathed slowly and steadily as I tapped in the PIN number. The machine made a rude noise. "Incorrect PIN. Please try again."

I started to tap the keypad again, but thought better of it. I pressed the 'cancel' button and waited for my card to reappear. And waited. After several seconds I pressed Cancel again. No card. I stared at the screen. Finally a message appeared.

"This card has been reported stolen. It has been confiscated. If you believe this is an error, please contact our Customer Service Department between 9 a.m. and 3 p.m. PST Monday through Friday. Thank you."

No money. And now no card.

How long would that $237.11 have to last?

In a sudden spasm of anger I kicked the ATM kiosk.

"Now, now, no need to wreck the machine before the rest of us get our money out," said a deep voice behind me.

I whirled around. The speaker was a man about my age, dark hair with graying temples, rimless glasses that he peered over to inspect me. He wore a neatly pressed Pendleton shirt tucked into comfortably worn jeans, and a humorous expression. Central casting could put him into a cowboy movie, or dress him in a tux and have him sidekick James Bond. "I—it—my card got eaten," I blurted.

"Bummer," he said. "Do you need anything to keep going until you can get it back again?"

Wow, I thought, what a nice guy.

"I just got to town and my—the place I was supposed to stay fell through," I admitted. "I don't have a lot of cash. I don't suppose you know of a cheap but decent motel? That allows dogs?"

He gave me a searching look. "Welllll...cheap but decent is kind of hard to come by these days. Even indecent will eat up your cash. But—" He chewed thoughtfully on his lower lip, looking me up and down. "How about this. We've got a little guest cottage at the back of our yard. Well, it's hardly a cottage, used to be a shed until the wife made me fix it up. It's just a bed and a chair and a little bathroom, but you'd be safer than in some fleabag motel with hookers and drug deals going on in the other rooms."

I stared at him in astonishment. "Are you serious? Why would you offer a stranger on the street a place to stay?"

"Because if my wife were stranded in some strange town without much money I would hope someone might give her a hand."

"But I—"

"Oh, come on. It's just a roof over your head that no one else is using tonight. Tell you what. I know my wife will force you to have dinner with us. You can do the dishes. Our house is old and there's no dishwasher. And she would kill me if she found out I let you wander off alone and friendless."

Something in me said say no, this is a bad idea. Something else said why not say yes?

"Besides," he added, looking over at my car where Clover had her paws on the steering wheel and looked ready to drive the Indy 500, "you've got that clearly vicious dog to protect you."

I laughed. "Okay. Yes."

3

His name was Darren Banfield. I followed him to his house, in a neighborhood of old homes just south of downtown. We stopped in front of a little cottage with a wide front porch. He must have phoned home while driving; a woman came out on the porch as soon as we pulled up and got out of the car.

"Beth, this is my wife Lisa." He reached over and gave her a quick kiss. She was a few years younger and a foot shorter than him, with shoulder length hair sporting honey streaks that told me she had a very skillful hairdresser. I received a narrow-eyed look when he introduced me, but she melted the instant she saw Clover.

"Oh, what a gorgeous thing you are!" She dropped to her knees and held out a hand for Clover to sniff, and was rewarded with a happy grin and wild tail wagging. "Is she—she?—still a pup?"

"No, but everyone thinks she is. She's nearly four but she's got that baby face. Careful, you'll have your face washed in a minute."

"Oh, I love doggy kisses." She proffered her cheek to Clover and giggled at the resulting smooch. "That's funny that everyone thinks she's a pup. Our dog is just the opposite." She sprang back to her feet in a manner I could only envy. "He's only five but everyone thinks he's an old man. They'll get along great."

"I told Beth you'd kill me if I left a lady stranded in a strange town," Darren told her.

"Absolutely." Her decisive nod made her silky, perfectly cut hair slide forward and back. "Stone cold dead. Good thing you agreed, Beth, or I'd be a widow by now. Come on, let me show you the shed."

"I thought we were supposed to call it the guest cottage," her husband grinned at her.

"Oh, shoot. Of course you are. 'Shed' just slips out after calling it that for the past twelve years."

She led the way into their house, which probably dated to the 1930s. The tidy living room was furnished with sleek Scandinavian pieces. We turned right through an arched doorway into the dining room, then into a galley kitchen with glass-fronted cabinets painted white and red tiled countertops. There was a built-in breakfast nook with upholstered benches beyond the kitchen, and a paned back door leading to the yard.

We stepped off the back stoop onto the lawn, and Lisa paused to say, "The yard is fenced if you want to let Clover off her leash. And Chester is out here somewhere."

In fact I had already spotted the figure of a dog, recumbent on its side in a sunny spot halfway down the long property. Clover walked a few steps away, gave some preliminary sniffs at the grass, then peed on what she deemed the perfect spot. Business taken care of, she trotted over to the other dog. He was so still that I hoped he hadn't passed away in his sleep. Such a tragedy would make it impossible for us to stay and witness his owners' grief.

But all was well. His tail began to thump lazily when Clover sniffed his head, then he opened his eyes and lumbered to his feet. He towered over Clover as they touched noses and performed other ritual greetings, then he slowly made his way up the yard to greet me. His wavy black fur was brushed with gold at the cheeks and toes, and he had charming golden eyebrows. His butt collapsed into a sit, and he offered me a paw and a beseeching look.

A laugh tumbled out of me as I took the paw. "Good afternoon, Chester, so nice to meet you."

Clover bustled over and inserted herself between me and the other dog, wagging and ducking her head.

"Don't worry, baby girl, you're still my bestie. But we need to be polite to Chester, this is his yard."

Lisa led me down a path toward the back of the property, past long perennial borders and a variety of trees. The garden shed—guest cottage—was tucked into the left back corner of the lot, under tall sheltering fir trees. As we neared our destination she said, "I hope you're not superstitious. That fence is between us and the cemetery."

"Really? Are the residents particularly rowdy?"

"Not so much. They're actually the quietest neighbors we've ever had."

"Perfect. I've lived a pretty quiet life, I should fit right in."

A rusty skeleton key hung next to the door of the little building, which clearly was a tarted up garden shed. But when she unlocked the door and pushed it open, I gasped with delight. It was about the coziest place I'd ever seen. To the right of the door, a paned window stood open over a small sink tucked into a short counter. Beyond the sink, there was room for a microwave and a toaster, and under the counter stood a dorm-sized refrigerator. The opposite back corner had been walled off into a tiny bathroom, complete with a glass-enclosed shower. To the left of the door, an overstuffed chair upholstered with flowered chintz stood near a day bed covered in the same fabric. A skylight in the middle of the ceiling made the tiny place glow with the pink-gold light of the setting sun.

"Lisa, Darren, this is *so* wonderful. I'd spend all my time here if this were my place."

"We hang out here quite a lot in the summer," Lisa said.

"Or when one of us is mad at the other," Darren added. "Then we call it the dog house."

"Well, my dog and I thank you so much. I'm sure I'll be able to get everything figured out tomorrow, but it's such a relief to have a safe place to stay tonight."

"Don't plan to rush off," Lisa said. "I've made the most enormous batch of macaroni and cheese you've ever seen and you're going to have to commit to helping eat it up."

"Mmmm, my fave."

She looked around the space, smoothed a little wrinkle from the bedspread, and poked her head in the bathroom. "Okay, towels are in the cupboard, coffee and tea stuff by the microwave. Holler if you need anything. Do you have much to bring in from the car?"

"Just one suitcase and some dog supplies."

"I'll help bring those in," Darren volunteered. "Come on, let's get you settled and then you can come help make salad. Just the thought of that macaroni and cheese has me drooling like Chester at Thanksgiving."

Conversation at dinner included more laughter than I would have believed possible after the day I had endured. The Banfields had lived all over the country, finally settling in Salem to put down some roots.

Darren said he was a consultant. Before he could elaborate, Lisa told me she designed gardens.

"It's a nice size town," she said. "Not too big or small, close enough to Portland to do stuff but without enduring the daily traffic they've got now. And we have what might be the best dog park anywhere."

I sat up straighter. "Really? Oh, that is great. When I was thinking about coming here I checked for dog parks and saw there are a few, but you never know what one is really like until you see it."

"Wait till you see Chester down there. He's a different dog." Lisa smiled at the two dogs, lying side by side a few feet away.

"Hey, Clover," Darren said, patting his thigh. "Come see what I've got in my pocket."

Wagging, she complied and wolfed down the treat he handed her. Chester noticed what was happening and heaved himself to his feet. Handing the black dog another treat, he added, "Yeah, he's a different dog, all right. He wakes up so he can mooch treats from everyone."

"Clover needs a lot of exercise or she's totally squirrely," I said. "Fortunately she'll retrieve for hours so it's pretty easy to keep her happy."

"I'll take you down there tomorrow," Lisa promised. "You know, we—" she waved her hand back and forth between her husband and herself— "actually met at a dog park."

"In D.C.," Darren added.

"Only he cheated."

"How do you cheat at a dog park?"

"By showing up with a borrowed dog, that's how."

"I had to," he protested. "I was walking by the park and I saw this really cute woman with a really cute dog and it was that thing you hear about. I took one look and knew this was the woman I was going to marry."

"Oh yeah, you say that *now*," she teased.

"So I watched what was going on in the park for a few minutes and saw this poor dog with a tennis ball. He kept dropping it at his owner's feet, but the guy was talking to someone and just ignored his dog. So I went in and asked if I could throw balls for his dog for a while. I said that I'd recently lost my own dog and I really missed playing fetch."

Lisa rolled her eyes. "Can you believe that? Making up a dead dog?"

"Not everyone is as cynical as you, you hard-hearted woman. Of course the guy said yes, and I worked my way over to that cute woman I'd spotted and struck up a conversation."

"Oh god, Beth, you would have cracked up. He thought he was being so nonchalant and sneaky, insinuating himself into my good graces. I asked him what his dog's name was, and he had to make something up. Sparky, he said. Sparky, I ask you! This was the last dog anyone on earth would ever have named Sparky—"

"It's all I could think of on the spur of the moment," her husband protested. "I actually thought it was pretty good. Better than, I don't know, Brownie."

"The really ridiculous thing was that I knew perfectly well whose dog it was. Everyone there was a regular except this guy throwing balls for Bruno the mastiff mix. Sheesh. Sparky."

They grinned affectionately at each other.

"How about you, Beth, you married? Divorced? Widowed? All of the above?" Darren asked.

"Darren! Geez, have you no manners? Ignore him, Beth."

Darren put on a hurt expression. "What did I do?"

22

"You wait until you've known someone for at least an hour before you start asking personal questions." She turned to me. "What he probably really wants to know is if you had a husband who left a lady stranded at an ATM and you had to kill him when he got home."

I pasted on a smile. "Actually, none of the above. I've lived a...a rather secluded life. Quiet but happy. My sister Georgette lived close by and we always had a good time together. But she died a while back." Inwardly I congratulated myself on how steadily I said that. I'd had to practice. "I finally decided it was time to see something of the world."

"I'm so sorry for your loss," Lisa said simply. I bit my lip and nodded.

"Thanks. I really miss her. She was always the life of the party. But...well, you have to keep going. Then I got the chance to come to Oregon. I totally felt like a pioneer woman crossing the country to a place that seems so exotic to me."

"Hmmm, exotic? Salem? Hope you think so in a year," Lisa said.

"Or a week," Darren added. She smacked his arm.

"Stop that. You love Salem and you know it."

"I do. I really do." His serious expression was clearly a struggle to maintain, and she whapped him again.

"Behave yourself," she commanded. "Come on, let's clear the table and we can all pitch in on the dishes."

"I promised I'd do the dishes in return for a bed for the night."

"Yeah, but the rule around here is, if you don't help with the dishes, you don't get dessert."

Darren jumped to his feet. "I'm helping," he announced, and began to gather plates.

4

As much as I wanted to head straight to the dog park with Clover in the morning, I knew I needed to discover the depth of the disaster my life had become before I did anything else. Lisa volunteered to keep an eye on my dog while I was gone, so I left Clover happily chewing on a Nylabone in a sunny patch of the yard, next to a sleeping Chester.

I reached the bank a few minutes after it opened. It was modern in a high-ceilinged, angular furniture sort of way, and brightly lit with morning sun slanting in through the huge plate glass windows. All burglaries in this bank were going to be on full display of anyone passing by.

Robbery, however, was not on my agenda. As I stepped into the lobby, I hoped I'd get my life sorted before I had to resort to anything like that. I asked the first person I saw sitting behind a desk if I could speak to the manager.

"Of course, ma'am." She stood, tucking a strand of her chin length bob behind an ear. With her neat sweater, knife-pleated skirt, dark tights and low shoes she could have passed for a Sixties schoolgirl. "Come with me, please."

She led me to a corner desk, larger than the others in the room but equally exposed. "Mr. Blaisdell, this lady asked to speak with you."

"Thank you, Brandy." He barely glanced up from the computer screen that held his attention. His tone was dismissive. Brandy immediately turned to go, leaving me standing in front of his desk. In the same tone he said to me, "What seems to be the problem?"

I've always found it interesting how some people can manage to irritate the life out of me within seconds of meeting them. Mr. Blaisdell had reached the level of manager at quite a young age, not much over thirty. I didn't care for his tone of voice to a stranger, a woman clearly his senior, and a customer, or that his focus remained on the computer screen. But what really got to me was the oh-so-carefully groomed scruffy beard and tiny mustache.

I waited until he finally looked at me, and raised an eyebrow at him. After a long enough pause for him to pay attention, I asked mildly in my best North Carolina accent, "May I be seated, sir?"

"Oh, um, yes, of course." I was pleased to hear from his tone that some of the wind had gone from his self-inflated sails. "What, er, how can I help you?"

"Your ATM machine ate my card yesterday. It did not recognize my PIN, even though I have used it many times before. I need to ascertain what has gone wrong and have the matter rectified."

"It could be something as simple as a damaged strip on the card. May I see some identification please?"

I handed him my billfold opened to my North Carolina driver's license. He glanced from it to my face, jotted down my name on a piece of scratch paper, and gave me back the billfold.

He set to work on his computer. A frown soon fixed itself on his face. He tapped more keys and the frown deepened. At last he looked back up at me. "I'm sorry, but I find no record of any account for you."

"I beg your pardon?"

"There is no account, of any kind, in your name. Could you have opened it in another name? Maybe you've been married or divorced since you opened it?"

"Young man, I have used the same name my entire life."

"Oh. Of course. Well, when did you last use your card? Before yesterday, I mean."

"I last accessed the account in Boise, Idaho when I withdrew cash from an ATM outside their downtown branch of this bank. I *do* have an account with your bank, sir. In fact, I have a savings account as well as checking, and they both have healthy balances in them."

Probably no one ever called him sir. It seemed to unnerve him. "Um, well, er, I see that your driver's license is from out of state. Maybe you have the wrong bank? I mean, there are several banks, national banks, with similar names. Like, um, Bank of America and U.S. Bank and—"

"Young man, I know perfectly well the name of the bank I have used for the past twenty-two years." I love calling someone 'young man.' I am instantly elevated to the power level of their grade school principal.

"Well, do you have your checkbook with you? That would definitely help."

I kept my expression the same, but inwardly that was the moment I got really scared. I rarely used my checkbook any more, just the credit and debit cards. So I had packed away my checkbook with my other financial records into a lockbox, which had been loaded onto a moving van. The contents of which had *not* been unloaded in the apartment for which Madam Blue Hair refused to give me a key.

A cold shiver of dread crawled up my spine. All of my belongings were gone. Someone claiming to be me had driven away with them several days ago. Aside from the items I had put into a storage facility back home, everything I still possessed was either on my back, in my car, or in the little guest shed at the back of Lisa and Darren's garden, just over the fence from the graveyard.

Do not panic, I told myself sternly. You still have most of the contents of your house locked up in that storage unit. Just deal with the checking account for now.

"No," I finally managed to say. "My checkbook is in transit from North Carolina."

"Oh. Of course. Well, as soon as it gets here, bring it into the bank and we can try again. You—you can ask for me personally. Oh, wait. Let me check one more thing."

He returned to his computer and tapped away. Tapped some more. Frowned deeply at the monitor.

"Ummm, according to our records, Beth Harding closed both a savings and a checking account last Thursday."

"What? What do you mean, closed them?" I knew it was a stupid question, but it blurted out on its own.

"I couldn't find the accounts earlier because I wasn't looking in the closed accounts, just the live ones." He shifted his eyes from the monitor to stare at my face. I could practically see the little wheels in his brain turning as he tried to work out what I might be up to.

I stood, and waited until it occurred to him that he should do the same. I reached across the desk and shook his hand. "Thank you for your assistance. Good day."

"Um, er, yes, good d—"

I turned and walked to the door. As I passed the young woman who had led me to his desk, I saw that she was studiously not looking at me. I stepped out onto the sidewalk.

Great. Mr. Scruffy Beard was doubtless even now putting information into the bank's computer that an imposter had tried to access some accounts that were recently closed. I was sure I had been caught on whatever security cameras they used. I wanted to run back to my car, half expecting to hear police sirens any moment, but forced myself to walk at a moderate pace. I started the engine and backed onto the street, then drove a couple of blocks until I saw another parking place and pulled in.

So what about the police? I'd always been law abiding and grew up believing that meant the police would be on my side. I had identification in my purse. And even though they were far away, dozens of people back home could vouch that I was indeed Beth Harding.

But going to the police would pry the lid off the box of secrets I carried within me. And that could be more dangerous than the identity theft. I was caught up in a game of cat and mouse, and my only safety lay in the cat being unaware of how much the mouse knew about what was going on.

One more question mark remained. I was sure I knew the answer, but I needed to be certain. I pulled out my cell phone and stared at it. I only carry a cell for emergencies, buying minutes for it when I run low. I had added several hours' worth before starting out on my journey. One more account that someone else must have access to. With shaking hands I checked the account balance, and breathed a sigh of relief when I saw it was what I remembered it should be. I dialed the number I'd memorized during several phone interviews.

"Good morning, Willamette Environmental Taskgroup Corporation, how may I direct your call?"

"May I speak to Beth Harding, please?"

"Just one moment, please." The same bland music I remembered from my interview calls began to play, but only a few bars had gone by when I heard a click. "This is Beth Harding, how can I help you?"

I clicked my phone shut and took a deep breath. Whoever she was, she had everything. My belongings, my job, my name, my money. I knew nothing about her except for one thing.

I have a very good ear for accents.

Her Southern accent was a fake.

5

The dog park was everything Lisa and Darren had said and more. I have no skill at estimating size, but the main field looked to be several acres, and there was a walking track around an equally large area of rough ground. A dissecting path led back into the woods. Trails meandered off into other areas of the park, but Lisa had warned me that past a certain point dogs needed to be on leash.

This was the only unfenced dog park I had ever seen, but it was so large that it would be a rare dog that would feel the need to go off-reservation.

Clover loved it.

She shot out of the car as soon as I released her, followed more slowly but just as eagerly by Chester. His owners had gladly accepted my offer to bring him along. After a quick stop at the poop bag dispenser, I followed them, smiling at a few other dog owners as I went.

Clover is a spaniel mix; her mother was a prized Springer and Brittany cross well known for her abilities in the field. Her papa was a traveling man, as they say, most likely short-haired since she is so sleek, and probably the contributor of her unflagging retrieving instincts. She has a particular ball that she loves; she doesn't share it, she doesn't lose it, and she will retrieve it for hours.

I made as long a throw as I am able (translation: not terribly far even with the Chuckit) and off she dashed, anticipating the ball's course and arriving at the bounce point a moment before it touched down. Back she came, I threw again. As we played I moved down toward the center of the field, keeping an eye on Chester.

He too was in his element, though running for a ball had no part in his dog park activities. There were perhaps ten people in sight with their dogs, most walking on the track around the rough ground. One by one he greeted every dog politely with nose sniffs and gently wagging tail. He then moved in front of each person, sat down, and gazed up at them expectantly.

It worked every time. The ones who already knew him cried, "Chester! Good boy! Do you want a cookie?" A couple of folks looked over at me and called, "Can I give him a treat?" To which I nodded and waved. He happily accepted each offering as well as any petting that came his way. Then he moved on to the next dog and owner. When everyone had been greeted (and sustenance provided) he trotted over to me and collapsed at my feet.

I'm not sure what I would have done that morning without those dogs. Bringing them to the dog park gave me a feeling that at least a little normality was left in my life.

I had spent my whole life sheltered in the familiar. Except for boarding school and college I had lived in the same house I was born in, and though my sister had been my only close friend, it was rare for me to see a face I did not recognize. I could have walked around my house and property blindfolded, and Georgette's as well.

Now it seemed that my only tether to this world was Clover. I snagged the ball she dropped at my feet and threw it into a patch of tall grass so she could have the fun of hunting it down.

And knew that I too must become a hunter.

"Hi! Isn't that Chester? Where's his owner? Sorry, I can't remember her name."

I'd been so intent on Clover I hadn't even noticed the woman approaching. Chester climbed to his feet to greet her and she gave him a small bone-shaped biscuit. She was small, her delicate face friendly under long dark hair intriguingly and liberally streaked with white. "Good boy, Chester, you old dog." She scratched behind his ears and thumped him on the shoulder. His hind end sank into a sit and he leaned against her.

"Yes, that is indeed Chester. Lisa let me borrow him."

"Lisa, that's right. I can remember dogs' names but people, not so much. I'm Janie—" she looked around and pointed to a Beagle— "and that is Tuffy. Tuffy!" she yelled. He glanced her way but kept following his nose across the field. She shrugged and turned back to me. "Oh well. He'll be back."

I smiled at her nonchalance. "I'm Beth, and this is Clover." She was back again with the ball, but dashed away as I scooped it up for another throw.

"I can see she's very focused," Janie nodded. "Tuffy may be my natural child, we both have the attention span of an adolescent squirrel. Have I seen you here before?"

"No, we just got to town yesterday." Another throw of the ball. "So far it's been a total screw up, but at least the dog park is great."

"Why? What happened?"

"Oh, the place I was going to live in fell through." Was there anyone I could trust? I could feel paranoia settle on my shoulders like a smothering shawl. "And, um, I had a job lined up and they seem to have given it to someone else."

"Oh my god, you poor thing. And you just came to town yesterday? That was a seriously bad day."

Another ball throw. "Seriously," I agreed.

"Do you have family here? Friends?"

I shook my head. "I met Chester's owner Darren yesterday afternoon by the ATM that ate my debit card."

"Wow, it just gets better and better, doesn't it?"

"Yes indeed. One upside was that he and Lisa were nice enough to give me a bed for the night, as well as feed me. But I can't abuse their hospitality. I've got to find some kind of job, any kind of job, and a place to stay."

Tuffy followed his nose back to Janie and paused to sniff my shoe, then greeted Chester. "Welcome back," Janie told him. "Do you want a cookie?"

He did, as did Chester. They gobbled down the crunchy treats she pulled out of a pocket. Then Tuffy was off again, nose to the ground. "If he could talk I bet he could name every person and every dog that's been here in the past month," Janie commented.

Since Chester was already standing, he deemed it a good opportunity to make his rounds again. I watched his technique with admiration. If people didn't already have his treat ready when he ambled up, he sat down in front of them and simply stared until they obeyed his mental command. You could practically see the thought-balloon over his head that said, "*Give the dog a cookie...give the dog a cookie...*"

Janie was watching him as well. "You've got to hand it to him. He really knows what he's doing."

"Maybe he can give me some pointers, in case I get to the begging-on-street-corners stage."

"No, no, wait!" she chided. A smile lit up her face. "I have a much better idea. I mean, unless you have some incredible and sought-after skills that will land you a high-paying job by Tuesday?"

"It seems unlikely."

"Or maybe you actually *want* to stand on a street corner with a sign?"

"It's not on my bucket list."

"Can you do stuff like run a washer and dryer and dust?"

"You need a maid? I've never done that but I have taken care of my own house."

"No, no, okay I wish I had a maid but doesn't everyone? But no. Here's the deal. I own a thrift store downtown, and my son Jasper has been helping me run it, and he just went off to college. He's been gone two weeks and I'm already drowning in donations and the place is starting to look like some demented hoarder's warehouse instead of a place normal people might actually want to shop."

"You have a thrift store?"

I actually love a good thrift.

"I do, for my sins. People donate because we support a couple of animal rescues. And the other part is, I live over the store. It's actually two little apartments, and I let Jasper have one of them for his own place which he thought made him the coolest kid in high school."

"That has to be every high schooler's dream, their own apartment."

Clover returned and lay down at my feet. She carefully placed her ball between her front legs, then panted happily.

"Hey, Clover—Clover, right?—hey sweetie, you want a cookie?" Janie offered her a treat, which she delicately accepted. "What a good girl. You'll want to hear this too. I'm telling your mom something to make up for yesterday."

Clover thumped the ground with her strong tail. Janie looked back at me.

"So anyway, like I said, Jasper left for college. In Vermont, can you believe that? Too far away to come home until Thanksgiving. So his place is empty."

"But Janie, you can't just take in—"

"Of course I can. I'm an eccentric who runs a thrift store. I can do anything I damn well please."

"I admit I've always appreciated a good eccentric."

"I can't afford to pay you much, but if you'd be okay with room and board in exchange for—how do they put it?—light duties in my store, it would mean you won't have to stand on street corners with a sign saying your dog will chase balls for food."

"I can't believe you want to take a total stranger into your home. This is twice in two days people have offered me a place to stay. Is it a town tradition or something?"

"Oh, yes. Everyone in Salem takes in strangers all the time. In fact, we compete to see who found the most interesting stranger of the month. There's a prize."

I laughed. Clover took it as a sign she should retrieve some more throws. She jumped up, dropped her ball on my foot, and ran out into the field. I threw it, then looked around for Chester. He was still soliciting, so I turned back to Janie.

"I'm afraid you won't win any prizes for me."

38

"That's okay. I won last month. I found a Russian basketball player who had been kicked off his team for distilling vodka in the locker room and then refusing to share with the other players."

"That does sound prize worthy."

"I had to let him go though. He kept bashing his head on the door frames."

"But your store. I could rob the till or something."

She snorted. "Okay, in the first place, there's usually so little in the till that you'd probably do better with the sign on the street corner. And it all goes to support homeless puppies and kitties. That's right, orphans. Little furry orphans. A dog person like you rob the till?" She shook her head. "I don't think so." After a pause she added, "Of course if you're a serial killer the deal is off. Are you?"

"A serial killer? Only of flies and mosquitoes."

"Around here you'll have to add ants to your list. Oh, you can't be a terrorist either. Okay?"

"No, I have no interest in terrorism. We're good there."

"Great! So will you help me out? It really will be a huge help, and it will give you a chance to look for a real job. Say you will."

I looked her in the eyes, and as paranoid as yesterday had made me, I could see nothing there but honest good will. I took a deep breath.

"Okay. Yes. And thank you."

6

Lisa knocked on the garden-cottage door a few minutes before six that evening. "I hope you don't mind leftovers," she said. "I did warn you about the size of that casserole."

"It was delicious last night and will be even better tonight."

"Probably will at that. Come on up to the house whenever you're ready. Darren just got home so we can all pitch in on the salad making."

"I'll come now." I followed her out of the guest shed and up the garden path. "I hope you had a good day. Chester had a great time at the dog park."

"He's probably comatose from all the treats he was given."

"Oh, yes. Comatose but happy. And everyone seemed so happy to see him."

"He is a pretty popular guy," she admitted. We reached the back door and she held it open for me. The kitchen was warm, and a tray of fresh baked muffins sat on the counter. I gave an appreciative sniff.

"Mmmm, muffins."

"And she is the muffin queen," Darren said, coming in from the dining room. "Hey, Clover! Did Chester show you the park?"

She wagged at him, and he pulled a small dog biscuit out of his pocket and tossed it in her direction. She caught it, crunched twice, and gave him her best winsome look.

"Oh, okay, one more," he said. To me he added, "I think Chester's been giving her some tips."

We busied ourselves constructing a large green salad, then Darren pulled the mac and cheese from the oven. Once we were at the table he asked, "Everyone have a good day? Beth, how did it go at the bank? Did you get everything squared away?"

Once again I struggled with how much to reveal. Part of me wanted to confide everything to these kind people. But my habit of reticence was long established. I wonder how differently things might have turned out if I had been more forthcoming.

I gave him a smile and said, "It's not quite all fixed, but I'm sure it will be soon. Meanwhile, I had a bit of luck at the dog park."

"Really? Oooh, tell me you found a bag of money or something." Lisa's eyes shone with the fantasy.

"I wish." I shook my head. "But maybe the next best thing. Do you know Janie? Gosh, I don't know her last name."

"No one does down there," Lisa assured me. "Which dog is hers?"

"Tuffy. He's a beagle."

"Oh yes, the woman with the streaky hair."

"That's right. Well, she runs a thrift store downtown—"

"I think I knew that. Darren, is that the one that supports a couple of animal groups? Rescues?"

He shrugged. "No idea."

"That's right, she mentioned that. When she heard about what happened yesterday, she offered to trade me room and board for help in the store while I look for a real job. Her son has just gone off to college, so his room will be vacant until Thanksgiving."

For a moment, I felt a stillness in the room, as though someone had opened a freezer door. Then it was gone. I thought I must have imagined it.

"How perfect!" Lisa beamed. "Almost as though it were meant to be."

"We don't want you to rush off," Darren said.

"You've been more than kind," I assured him. "I'm not sure where I'd have ended up last night if you hadn't rescued me."

"I was actually rescuing the ATM machine that you were bent on destroying." He gave me a cocky smile.

"It's lucky for you guys. One more night of your delicious food and you'd have a boarder for life. You'd be plotting how to get rid of me."

"It's been delightful to get to know you," Lisa assured me. "I'm sure we'll see you often. You'll discover that Salem is actually not a very big town. And look, you've fulfilled your duty." She spooned a last dollop of macaroni on each of our plates. "We said you had to stay to help finish this, and you did."

In the morning I loaded my few belongings into the car, tidied up the tiny guest house and wrote a thank you note on a card I'd purchased the day before. I tucked it under the vase of flowers I'd picked up at the same time. One last glance around, then I hung the skeleton key on the nail where Lisa had gotten it yesterday. They were both already gone for the day so we had said our farewells last night. Now I put my purse in the car and strapped Clover into her seat, and we were off.

I fell in love with Janie's thrift store the instant I walked through the door. I was already smiling at the name—"Pick of the Litter"—and then the atmosphere of the place grabbed me. I hadn't felt so at home since I'd crossed the county line six miles from where I was born and headed west. I glanced down at Clover and saw she had her head up and was sniffing the air like a connoisseur.

"You're here! Hooray!" Janie hurried up the center aisle with the arms outstretched. The hug she gave me made my eyes sting with gratitude.

"I. *Love*. This. Store," I said. "I've been here two seconds and already I love it."

"You'll love it more when it's not such a mess."

"Oh, pooh, you have awfully exaggerated ideas of what a mess is."

"Trust me, this is a mess."

"I'll have to take you to the thrift store in Walnut Falls. About a hundred years ago it was a fabric store, one of those mill end places where bolts come in and never leave until some fool buys them. The tables holding the bolts got so full that part of the floor collapsed, and they just left it. Big old V in one aisle. Then it became a thrift store and all the thrift stuff just got piled on top of the old bolts of fabric."

"And the floor is still collapsed?" She looked horrified. I could see visions of liability claims dancing in her wide eyes.

"Sure is. Everybody just walk around it. One lady did fall and break her leg. Of course she was a tourist and didn't know about it. But they keep first aid supplies in the back room, so they patched her up and she was able to keep shopping."

"Beth, are you pulling *my* leg?"

"Heck no. That's exactly how I heard the story, and from a church lady so it had to be true."

"Well, I'm glad to say our floors are sound both down here and upstairs. I'd hate for my bed to go crashing through in the middle of the night and wake up among a lot of broken china. Or dead. So where are you parked? Want to bring your stuff in?"

"I got lucky, the car is right out front."

"Perfect. Let's tote everything up to your room, and then I'll show you where to park behind the building. And give you a remote for the gate to the parking lot. We share it with a couple other building owners."

We each grabbed an armload from my car, and she led me to a locked door behind the sales counter "I used to just leave this open," Janie explained, "until I heard noises overhead one day and found a woman up here making herself some breakfast."

"Seems a mite pushy."

"It was, as was the fact she was wearing my favorite cashmere sweater. I mean, we do welcome strangers here, but there are limits. So now we keep the door locked."

The stairs were steep and long, with oak treads that made satisfying creaks when stepped on. At the top was a short hallway with one closed door on each side. At the end of the hall, a curtained alcove held a large open sash window over a window seat padded with cushions.

"All my life I have wanted to live somewhere with a window seat," I breathed.

"Just shove Tuffy over when you want to hang out there. It's his favorite spot."

Tuffy had followed us up the stairs and now went straight to the window seat and hopped up. I unhooked Clover's leash. She went to the alcove and joined the other dog. They sat side by side and panted at us.

Janie shook her head. "I may faint from the cuteness."

Turning to the door on the left, she inserted a key in the lock over the knob. "I've been trying to air out the eau de teenage boy," she said over her shoulder as she pushed the door open and walked in. I followed, blinking in the bright light that streamed through the full length window in the front of the room "It got a lot better after I found and removed all the dirty gym socks."

In fact, while clearly the habitat of a teenage boy, the room was beautifully clean. Long and high ceilinged, the brick walls were painted a warm gray. A leather covered chair and footstool sat in the front corner by the window, next to one of those vintage floor lamps with a round table attached to the pole. A small bathroom had been enclosed in one back corner, and the other held a miniscule kitchen with sink, two burner gas stove, a little under-counter fridge, and some cupboards. The long wall opposite the door had four small windows near the ceiling, under which was mounted a large flat screen television. Industrial looking shelving made of planks and pipes surrounded the screen. An open door on the long, low cabinet underneath the TV showed empty hangers on a rod, indicating it served as closet space.

On the other long wall, a tidy metal desk and rolling chair occupied the space under a raised platform bed. A large black and white poster of the moon's surface hung over the desk. The stretch of exposed wall between the left end of the bed and the bathroom had been turned into a climbing wall, with colorful holds mounted all over it.

"Um, Janie, do I have to climb up the wall like some superannuated cat burglar in order to go to bed?"

She laughed. "You should see your face. That actually is how my son went up and down, but for us old ladies, we have this." She gestured to the other end of the bed structure, and I was relieved to see a bright red metal spiral staircase.

"Whew. Guess I can manage that, and even more importantly so can Clover. I hope you allow dogs on the furniture?"

"That is precisely why we installed it, so Tuffy could sleep with Jasper. Come on, let's get the rest of your stuff up here and let you settle in. You officially have today off but I warn you, tomorrow I turn into a slave driver." She led the way back down the stairs, asking over her shoulder, "Have you eaten?"

"I have, Lisa supplied me with cereal and milk and bread. So I'm good, thanks."

"Well, there's plenty of snack stuff in my kitchen, and I put a few things in yours as well. I thought we could rustle up some sandwiches for lunch, and I made a pot of minestrone yesterday."

"How did you know I love minestrone?"

"Oh good." We emerged at the bottom of the stairs into the store, and she closed the door behind me. "Have you ever noticed that it is impossible to make a

47

small batch of minestrone? I am so glad to have someone to help eat it."

"That is *exactly* what Lisa said about the macaroni and cheese she had made."

"Of course I've spent the last several years cooking for a bottomless pit and his friends. It takes a while to learn to scale back. Seriously, you showed up at exactly the right time. Hey, there's a job for you—we can hire you out to recent empty nesters to help them transition their cooking."

"Great idea. I'll be employed in no time."

"We'll make people submit samples of their cooking first. No need to accept any gigs from bad cooks."

Getting settled didn't take long. The limited wardrobe I'd packed for the car trip plus my truncated stay in the cabin on Mount Hood went straight into the washing machine, located downstairs in the staff area at the back of the store. Upstairs, I found that either Jasper had taken all his bathroom paraphernalia with him, or Janie had tidied away what he'd left behind. I had plenty of room for my bits and pieces. My laptop went on the desk, and I plugged the Kindle into its charger beside it.

Clover's water and food bowls fit nicely at the end of the kitchen counter, and her bin of kibble slid onto the bottom shelf in one of the cabinets with about an inch to spare. I peeked into the bin, saw there were enough of the brown bits to cover the bottom of the bin by several inches, and made a mental note to buy more soon.

Then I looked around for a good place to put the last item in my suitcase. Nothing immediately seemed right. I climbed up the spiral stairs to the loft bed with it in my hand. There I found that several bricks had been removed and lined with wood to make a little nook. A couple of books had been left there, *Ender's Game* and a technical-looking manual on astronomy. Above this recess a small brass light was built into the wall; it looked like something you'd see on a yacht. Just right for reading in bed.

I heard Clover's toenails click on the metal stairs, and in a moment she was beside me on the bed.

"Look, baby girl, here's the perfect place for our picture." I set the framed photo in the niche and gazed at it. My sister and me with Clover between us. We had found some of our grandmother's Sunday dresses and hats from the Fifties in a box in the attic and had spent the afternoon playing dress up like we had as children. We even had a tea party under the giant magnolia that shaded my side porch. When the mailman came by we'd asked him to take our picture. Once he stopped laughing he'd agreed.

It was the last picture taken of her before she died.

Clover can read my emotions as well as any professor ever read a textbook. She moved close and gave me a little smooch. I curled up on the very comfortable mattress and she settled in beside me, her chin resting on my arm. In a few moments we were both asleep.

"I don't know who was sounder asleep, you or your dog."

"Was I snoring terribly?"

"No, but your dog was."

I laughed, snagged the ball the Clover had dropped at my feet, and flung it across the dog park field. "She does snore, for sure. You'd think she was a pug or a bulldog to hear her."

"It really warmed the cockles of my heart. She sounded exactly like my son Jasper. I just can't believe my good luck in finding the two of you. Help in the store, your dog snores like my son, you ate not one but two bowls of soup, and if that weren't enough those biscuits you made for dinner were to die for. I'm pretty sure when Jasper comes home he's going to have to look for another place to stay, because you're feeling like a keeper."

"Just wait till all my irritating habits start to emerge. I have a feeling Jasper's place is safe."

I picked up Clover's ball once more and started to throw it, then realized she was running toward the parking lot, tail wagging. She dashed up to a woman with a large black dog. I recognized Lisa and Chester, and when I waved they started our way. Lisa arrived first since Chester had to make a few stops to greet people and collect tribute.

"That dog," she laughed. "I don't know why I bother to feed him at home. He gets more than enough down here."

"Lisa, I think you know Janie, don't you?"

"Sure. How are you, Janie? How's the thrift store?"

"Oh, currently drowning in donations, but that's a good thing. How have you been?"

"Great. Really great. Darren's here somewhere, I think he stopped to talk to a crony. Or maybe he's mooching treats like Chester."

"Hmmm, I wonder if that's why my son used to volunteer to bring Tuffy down here. He was actually begging for treats since I never fed him enough."

"Well, if Salem runs out of crazy people willing to offer me a bed and a meal, I might try it too," I told them.

They both smiled. "No worries," said Lisa, "there are plenty of crazy people in a town this size. After all, it's the state capitol. There must be an untold number of crazy politicians."

"And many of them shop at my store, so you're safe. Crazy people, that is. I'm not sure how many of them are politicians."

Another couple with a young black standard Poodle came up to us then, people that Lisa knew, and the conversation became general. I answered a few questions about where I'd come from and my trip west, and then the dogs claimed our attention. Darren ambled up and said something about a duck's game. The conversation became incomprehensible. Janie noticed my blank expression. She leaned over and said quietly in my ear, "Football. College. The Oregon Ducks. You'll also hear about the Beavers, the OSU team."

"Thanks," I murmured back. "I don't do football."

"Me neither."

We exchanged conspiratorial smiles.

Clover finally decided she was sufficiently exercised and collapsed on my feet, panting. Darren grinned down at her. "I think you could use a few extra calories," he said, tossing her one of the little bone shaped treats he kept in his pocket. She ate it and rolled over on her back, wiggling and wagging.

The sun was about to dip below the trees at the west end of the field, and our shadows were long.

"We'd better head home," Janie said, looking around for her dog. "Tuffy! Tuuuufffy! Come on boy!" Tuffy emerged from behind a tall tuft of grass and came running. We said good night to the others and walked up the field to my car, loading the two dogs into the back seat. I'd come out without Clover's seatbelt, but we were only a couple of miles from home and I had the top up on the car. I wasn't worried.

We left the parking lot and headed up the curving road through the park. As we neared the traffic light at the main road, Janie asked, "Do you want to go straight home, or take a little drive along the river?"

"That would be great. I haven't seen anything of Salem yet."

"We'll just go a little ways. Turn right at the light."

I followed her instructions, smiling at her tour guide patter. "On our right, we are passing a large golf course. Which is of no interest to me because I do not play golf."

"Me neither."

"Oh good. Coming up now is the lovely building that houses my doctor's office, and soon, wait for it, yes—the charming Plaid Pantry for all your convenience store needs."

The road curved to the left, and I touched the brakes to take the bend a little slower. Nothing happened. Puzzled, I touched the brake pedal again. It went all the way to the floor, but the car didn't slow down. In fact it speeded up.

"And now, on our left, I know you will appreciate—"

"Janie!" My voice came out in a strangled squeak. "The brakes! They're gone!"

7

"Oh, very funny." She gave me a mock frown. "But there's a real curve coming up. Stop joking."

"I'm not joking." Talking through gritted teeth while guiding an uncontrollable car down an unfamiliar road with night about to fall was not the easiest thing I had ever attempted.

"What! Wait, maybe you accidentally pushed the gas, not the brakes." she cried.

"No. I didn't."

"What are we going to do?" she gripped her seat cushion with both hand. "Try the emergency brake!"

I reached down to the hand brake beside my seat and pulled it tentatively, then harder. It flew up with no resistance.

"Can you jump out?" I asked her.

"Hell no."

Our road had led out of town almost immediately, and at the moment no other cars were in sight. My heart was beating so hard I could barely breathe. But the adrenaline coursing through my system had the effect of making my vision crystal clear. Time stretched out and everything moved in slow motion.

My right hand flicked to the emergency flasher button on the dashboard. Then I began weaving across both lanes in wide swoops in an attempt to slow the car. It helped, but not enough. Our speed kept inching higher.

"Do a one-eighty! Like in all the cop movies!"

"Can't, that needs the emergency brake. Look for a field to drive into."

Janie suddenly pointed and shouted, "There!" I saw that she was right. Setting my jaw, I pulled the steering wheel hard to the right.

We flew off the road, sailing over a shallow ditch that would probably be a stream in the rainy season. The barbed wire fence we hit snapped like a thread, and then we were in the field and slowing down.

I wrenched the wheel to the right again, then took a deep breath and turned off the ignition. The steering column locked and we coasted in a circle. Slower. Slower. And finally stopped.

We were surrounded on all sides by baby Christmas trees. I was pierced with sadness that we'd had to kill so many of them.

Beside me Janie turned in her seat and gave me an open-mouthed stare, and then breathed out a heartfelt, "Holy crap."

"Yeah."

"I think I may throw up."

I looked over at her. "I—I would rather you didn't." My voice shook.

Tuffy stuck his head between our seats. Let's go! There are smells to be sniffed in that field!

"We should get out. We have to figure out what to do next." Pushing the release button on my seat belt was as much as I could manage at the moment.

"All the starch is gone from my knees." Janie pulled her door latch and pushed weakly. The door opened a couple of inches. But a couple of inches were invitation enough for Tuffy. Instantly he wiggled between the front seats and onto her lap, ready to leap out of the car. She grabbed for his leash. "Dammit, Tuffy, stop it. We've just survived a runaway car. All I need now is for you to run out on the road and get hit."

"Clover, wait," I commanded, and opened my own door a few inches.

And immediately smelled gasoline.

"Get out! I think the gas tank got punctured!"

We discovered that adrenaline could resurge in an instant and we tumbled out of the car. "Clover, here!" She flew to me and I grabbed her leash. We stumbled away, tripping over the closely planted knee high trees. Clover and I reached the road first and stopped, both of us panting. Janie straggled up, pulling Tuffy behind her with the leash. His nose was glued to the ground as he tried to inhale the scent of every bunny who had hopped through that field.

"Wow, what a nightmare," she gasped. We both looked back at the car sitting quietly with open doors in the middle of a zillion baby Christmas trees. "At least it didn't ex—"

And of course, that is exactly when it did explode.

It seemed like weeks later that we unlocked the front door of the thrift store and stumbled inside, though it probably was no more than an hour.

"I'm awfully glad we didn't have to walk home," I commented as we trudged wearily up the stairs.

"That's the advantage of staying put for over thirty years. Someone I knew was bound to come along."

In fact, quite a crowd had come along. The owner of the field lived down by the river, on the other side of his farm. "My god, am I glad I've got insurance," were his first words. And then, "Are you gals okay?"

The seemingly-empty road now produced a number of other cars, most of which stopped. Nearly everyone who got out to watch a convertible burning away to its carcass also asked if we were okay. Someone had the presence of mind to make a 911 call (neither Janie nor I thought of it). In a few minutes, a fire truck arrived and began their drill, moving people away and deploying equipment. As the sun finally set and darkness began to thicken, a couple of teenage boys who had arrived on a motorcycle offered to put flares on the road in both directions.

The sheriff's deputy who showed up had more searching questions about the accident. He looked amazingly like Tom Selleck, somewhere in age between the Magnum days and his role as the New York Police Commissioner. I wondered if this guy—the badge over his pocket said "Hayworth"—ever considered shaving off his heavy mustache.

"I don't suppose you rescued the registration or insurance information from the car before you left it?" His raised eyebrow seemed to indicate negligence on my part.

Part of my brain detached itself from the part that was in shock and did some fast thinking. This could be my chance, while I had the evidence of the tampered brakes to back me up, to tell the police about what was happening to me. I shoved Clover's leash into Janie's hand, turned and walked a few feet away, behind a teenage couple who had probably been parking nearby. Officer Hayworth followed me.

"Sorry, everything was in the car, including my purse with my driver's license. But I know the license number." I reeled it off from memory, wondering as I did so why I could remember that number but not all my passwords. "Oh, it's from North Carolina."

"I thought you had an accent."

"Yes. As do you. Anyway, I just got to town a couple of days ago. Listen, the brakes…the brakes wouldn't work. Emergency brake too."

"Sometimes we think we're pushing the brake when we're really on the accelerator."

"I'm sure that has happened, but it wasn't the case here."

"Uh huh. You don't say." His pursed lips showed he did not believe me. I wouldn't get any further by insisting that the car had been sabotaged. He busied himself filling out some kind of report form. At last he looked up.

"Well, it's a single car accident, so it's between you and your insurance company. And the guy who owns the trees, but I'm pretty sure Roger has insurance too."

Lisa was right, I thought. Salem really is a small town in disguise.

"You'll need the accident report to give to your insurer," he went on. "Should be available by tomorrow afternoon. Give us a call and we can fax it to you." He handed me a business card. "How can I reach you if I have any more questions? Cell phone?"

"It was in my purse." The thought of what I had lost began to overwhelm me, but I beat it back for the moment. Time to panic later. Then I decided to take a chance. "But I've just started a new job at Willamette Environmental Taskgroup. You can call the main switchboard and ask for Beth Harding."

"All righty then." He snapped his notebook closed. "Do you and your friend need a ride somewhere?"

I shook my head. "We'll be fine. I think she's found us a ride already."

He gave a short nod and returned to his car. In a moment he was gone.

I couldn't help the little glow of satisfaction I felt at having landed this particular mess in the lap of the woman pretending to be me.

"I don't know about you," Janie said as she unlocked her door, "but I need some alcohol. Wine or booze?"

"Let me feed Clover first. She didn't eat before we took them to the park."

"Oh. Right. Tuffy too. Okay, feed dogs, then booze. Come over when you're done."

I practiced deep cleansing breathing as I scooped food into Clover's bowl. I needed some time to think, but in mere moments her dish was empty. Since she'd been outside all evening, I decided I could wait to give her a final walk for the day.

I looked around Jasper's room that I had occupied for only a few hours, and realized I'd miss it as much as my North Carolina home. I hadn't even gotten a chance to try out the climbing wall.

"I'll have to leave tomorrow." I accepted the rather full glass of red wine that Janie handed me when I returned to her living room. I sank into the closest chair, an old wooden rocker.

"No, you're not." Her voice was matter of fact.

"There's no telling what will happen next. I can't bring my trouble into your life."

"That's what friends are for. Besides, you're not going anywhere until you tell me what is going on."

I shook my head. My lips folded in, locked together by fear.

"Beth, everyone has secrets. Lord knows I have a few and it would take more than a bottle of pinot noir to get them out of me. But I can see you're in trouble.

If you don't tell me at least part of it, I promise I will literally die of curiosity right here and now. Then you'll not only have the original trouble, but you'll have to figure out what to do with my body. *And* you'll have to pay my son's college tuition. Believe me, you do not want to take that on."

Something that was a cross between a laugh and a sob burst out of me. "Since my purse with all my money except for a couple of twenty dollar bills I had tucked into my sock drawer is now a pile of ash in a Christmas tree field, I don't think I can take on any more financial commitments at the moment."

"Right. Plus, you don't have any place to go, and no car to get there."

"This is getting very depressing."

"You're clearly a competent, educated, articulate person who is dealing with extraordinary circumstances. So sit there and drink your wine and think about what you're going to tell me while I grab some snacks. I don't know about you, but after that magnitude of fright, I need carbs."

Janie placed a tray of cheese, crackers and brownies on the coffee table between us, and settled into a corner of the sofa. "Okay, so yesterday at the park you told me that the job you had lined up fell through, as well as the place you were supposed to live," she prompted.

"Don't forget the ATM that ate my debit card. I don't know when I've had a more productive day."

"So start with the job. You got here and found out they'd withdrawn their offer?"

I took a deep breath. I had to go with my intuition, which told me that if I could not trust this woman who had taken me in, I could not trust anyone. What the hell, I thought. "Oh, it's way worse than that. Someone is pretending to be me, and she is working there."

"What!"

"Yeah. Okay, it started day before yesterday at breakfast. Actually, it must have started before that but I only stumbled over this—this plot then. Oh lordie, that sounds so paranoid. It *is* paranoid, but it still happened."

"Just because you're paranoid doesn't mean people aren't out to get you."

"So true. All right, at breakfast I tried to buy a book for my e-reader, and it wanted a password. Which it never asks for, the password was saved on the device. I had no idea what the password was for that particular site, but I figured I could look it up when I got back to where we were staying. I keep a list of all the umpty-dozen passwords I've acquired. Then when I used my credit card to pay for breakfast, it was refused."

"So before yesterday morning you had no idea that there was a problem with anything?"

"Right. Clover and I left North Carolina a couple of weeks ago. I wanted to see something of the country on the way here, I haven't traveled much. I used the credit card for all my hotel rooms and most meals, and got cash from ATMs when I ran low.

"I had found this little cabin on Mount Hood through Airbnb and decided to spend a week or so up there. A break to mark the end of my old life and the beginning of the new. I had put most of the stuff in my house into storage, and hired a moving company to pack up what I wanted to bring to Oregon. I found an apartment online and again used the credit card for the deposit and first month's rent. The movers were to deliver my belongings to the apartment, and I was supposed to pick up the key when I got to town from the apartment complex manager."

"You couldn't have been too paranoid a person when you made *that* plan," Janie said bluntly. "I could tell you tons of horror stories about moving companies. And the apartment could have been in a sketchy part of town."

"Hindsight being what it is, you're right. I should have stored everything and just picked up the basics once I got here. But—well, I needed some of my own stuff around me. Hard enough to start a new job in a new place where I knew no one."

"I can see that."

"So I rushed back to the cabin to check my password list. At that point I was still focused on buying a book to read. But when I found my password list, the password didn't work. *None* of my passwords worked."

"Someone stole your list."

"Which I truly believed I had kept hidden and safe."

"Man, I am going to go find my own list and copy it over in invisible ink."

"Good idea. Anyway, I was pretty freaked out. I threw everything in the car and left the cabin a day early and came rushing down to Salem. I went straight to the apartment complex. It was horrible. The manager yelled at me from an upstairs window that I had to be an imposter, because Beth Harding had arrived a few days ago, cancelled the apartment, and left with the moving van. She claimed she'd found another place to live and was willing to forfeit the deposit."

"Well, yeah, since it wasn't her money."

"I was getting beyond scared by now. I realized I only had a couple of hundred dollars left in cash, and no credit card that would work. So I found the closest ATM for the bank I've used for years. And it ate my card. Darren was waiting to use the ATM and saw me kick it—"

"I've often wanted to kick those things, and none has ever even eaten my card."

"Darren took pity on the sad story of my card being eaten, and that's how I ended up staying at their place. I'm still amazed that they, and you, actually invited me to stay."

"It's the Southern accent. I swooned the moment you opened your mouth. Really, you won't need money any more if you stay here. Everyone who hears your honeyed tones will be swept off their feet."

"Didn't seem to work on that cop." I brightened. "Maybe I could become a con artist."

"Ahhh." Her eyes danced as she leaned forward to snag a brownie. "Maybe you already are. But back to your story. What about the job? What kind of job, anyway?"

I wondered how little information I could get by with telling her.

"It was sort of a research position."

"And did they give it to another candidate, or to the woman who stole your moving van?"

"I think to her. I wasn't supposed to start until next week, but she must have showed up early saying she was me. I called and asked for Beth Harding, and they connected me with a woman who answered by that name. My name. In a bad fake Southern accent."

"But wait." She frowned. "Wouldn't the people who interviewed you realize she was a ringer?"

"The interviews were by phone. I never met them in person."

"I'm sure they would have checked out any pictures of you online. At least once they realized you were a serious candidate."

"I don't have much of an online presence." I had worked hard to keep it that way.

"Lucky you. If you Google my name you get shots of me playing kickball in a muddy field, and an assortment of mug shots of someone with the same name who went to prison for kiting checks. Here's another question: this thing that happened with the car tonight, the brakes failing. That wasn't an accident, was it?"

"No. I don't think so."

"So some woman, either working alone or with others, for an unknown reason unless it was just opportunistic, anyway some woman steals your identity, your job, your home, your belongings and your money, and tampers with the brakes on your car, and no one notices? Damn."

Clover chose that moment to wake up. She stood, stretched and gave her ears a good shake, then lay down again and emitted a heartfelt groan. We both laughed.

"You said it, Clover," Janie told her. Then she looked at me. "Okay. There's just one thing for us to do."

"What's that?"

"We are going to nail her ass."

8

Janie was positively perky the next morning. "I woke up with so many great ideas," she told me. "When you finish your breakfast, meet me downstairs. I'm going to start gathering some supplies from the store. Oh, and I've already taken both dogs out for a potty break."

Before I could utter a thank you, she was clattering down the wooden stairs. Definitely a morning person.

I scrambled an egg and ate it with a piece of whole wheat toast. Clover watched me with her bright hazel eyes, anticipating the moment when I handed her the crust. Then a quick brushing of the teeth, and I headed downstairs. Janie was in the back room, inspecting a faded red sweater.

"We've got over an hour before the store opens," she told me. "That's enough time to get started, and we can keep you mostly in the back here for now."

"What are we starting?"

"Your makeover." She waved the sweater she was holding at me. "Beth Harding is leaving town, going back to North Carolina. I'm putting her on the red eye from PDX tonight."

"Wait, what? You're sending me back? But—"

"I'm sending *Beth* back. *You* are about to become…what name would you like to use?"

"Janie! What? You're going to get some kind of black market ID?"

"No, no, well, maybe we could. I have no idea how you buy fake ID but probably anyone in the freshman class over at Willamette University could tell us. I just think you'll be safer if you're not you for a while."

"Okay," I said slowly, "I can see that. I might get away with no identification for a while."

"So what shall we name you?"

"How about Susie Strumpet?"

She choked on a laugh. "No! Be serious."

"I am. I've always thought Strumpet was a great name. Or Glockenspiel. Gloria Glockenspiel. That has a ring to it."

"Sure does, but I think we'd be better off going for something less memorable. Mary Smith."

"Mmmm, not Smith. It always sounds fake even when it's not. Johnson. And the rhythm of 'Mary' is better with another syllable…Mary Claire maybe."

"Mary Claire Johnson. I like it."

"My maternal grandmother was a Johnson."

"Perfect then. Goodbye Beth, hello Mary Claire. Now we have to find the perfect clothes to make you invisible."

"I've been invisible since I turned forty."

"I sure know that feeling. But let's not take any chances. Here, try this on."

She handed me a hunk of hair. I turned it a couple of different directions before discovering its true nature as a sort of tousled bouffant wig of mousy ash-brown. I wrinkled my nose.

"You want me to put this thing on my head?"

"It's clean. I know where it came from. Just try it."

I shrugged and pulled the thing over my own short hair. Janie fussed with it a bit, then handed me a pair of glasses. Large brown plastic frames from the Eighties. "Put these on. The prescription in them is pretty mild. You should still be able to see."

I donned the glasses. She looked at me and grinned. "Wow. Take a look."

She led me to a mirror hung on the wall near the washer and dryer.

I was unrecognizable. Even to myself.

"Good lord," I murmured. "If I didn't know that was me, I'd think it was Mary Claire Johnson."

Along with the wig I was issued a pair of brown slacks that were just slightly too short, a short sleeve cotton shirt in mustard yellow, and a stretched out, faded red cotton cardigan. Janie made me scrub off every stitch of makeup as well. She stepped back and gazed at me, admiring her handiwork.

"You look great!"

"I look like you know what."

"Yeah, but that's perfect. No one is going to look at you for one second longer than they have to."

"Wouldn't want to hurt their eyes. Tell me again why I am wearing this horrible outfit? Let me guess, you will never be able to sell any of this so you're pawning it off on me."

"Not at all. You may spark a new fashion."

"For what, ill-fitting clothes and bad color combinations?"

"Trust me, I've seen worse. And on some very rich people. As to why…let's just say I've got an idea. I'll need to make some phone calls to see if I can set it up. Meanwhile, we have one more problem to solve."

"Just one?"

"For now. Your voice. Your accent. Anyone who has heard you talk will know it's you."

For the first time in what seemed like years I was able to give a whole-hearted smile. "Would something along these lines work?" I said in my best Boston accent. Switching to Brooklynese, "Or maybe you like this better? What would a Mary Claire Johnson sound like?"

Her expression was akin to awe. "How do you *do* that?"

I shrugged. "It's just a knack. Some people pick up languages easily, I pick up accents."

70

"Now I'm starting to wonder if you actually *are* a con artist."

I spent the day in the back room, dividing my time between improving upon my disguise and working on some of the tasks I'd promised to do to earn my bed and board. There were boxes and bins of clothing to prep for the sales racks, plus every kind of houseware, toy and knickknack.

"Stick with the clothing for today," Janie instructed before going out to open the door to the public. "Anything that's too worn or torn to sell goes over here. Once a month we have a free-for-all where we sell it by the pound. It's become a very exciting contact sport."

"Maybe you could sell tickets for people to watch."

"I like the way you think. Then for pieces that are good enough to resell, the first thing is to give everything a quick sniff test. Anything smelly goes into the washer."

"Dry clean only?"

"Ah yes. I scrounged a big donation of those sheets that you use in the dryer. When there are enough pieces we do a load. The ones that are just a little off I hang back here and turn the fan on them to air. Stuff sells better if it smells okay, and I really don't want the store to have that famous thrift store pong."

"Gotcha."

"Everything goes on hangers on these racks. We'll let today's lot hang here until tomorrow so wrinkles can fall out. After a day or so, we use this steamer on

71

anything that's still wrinkled. Then we sort by type and size and they go out on the floor to find happy new homes."

I looked around. She hadn't been joking about the place looking like a hoarder's haven. "Should be enough to keep me busy for a while."

"Sisyphus would feel right at home here. Oh, one other thing. Keep an eye out both in the clothing and other donations for anything that looks really special. Sometimes we can make more by selling something online, or to a vintage dealer, and I've also got a special area for more expensive items. There's a list on the bulletin board over there of really high end brands and vintage designers."

"So, no bad smells and watch for buried treasure."

"Exactly. Okay, time to open the store. Holler if you need me. And stay out of sight!"

By the time the store closed at five-thirty, I was almost too tired to climb the stairs. I stood at the bottom looking up.

"Janie, why don't you move the store upstairs and live down here so we wouldn't have to climb all these stairs when I am so pooped?"

She gave me a little push. "You can do it. Come on, put one foot on the first step. Good girl, now the other foot on the next step."

Clover and Tuffy dashed by us to the top, then turned around to watch my slow progress.

"Show offs. Couldn't you at least have pulled me up with you?" I sighed and began the climb.

"You get used to it. And just think, at the top of those steps is food, wine, and a comfy bed."

I picked up my pace and finally reached the top. "I didn't realize what a cushy life I've been leading. I don't know when the last time was that I spent all day on my feet."

"You'll be a new woman tomorrow. Though come to think of it—" Janie paused to look me over— "you were a new woman today."

I pulled the wig off my head and gave my own hair a tousle. "Itchy."

"I've got a new package of knee high nylons. We'll make you a wig cap tonight. Let's go heat up the soup, shall we?"

"I'll be there in a minute. I want to put on my own clothes."

Clover followed me, looking hopeful. We'd only had two trips to the dog park, and she already considered it a routine. I quickly changed into jeans and an old sweater and led her out of Jasper's room and across the hallway to Janie's apartment. I found her in the kitchen stirring the pot of minestrone.

"I think we have a problem."

"Your life has been stolen and you only now think we have a problem?"

"Clover. She really needs exercise. I've never understood it myself since I can go for days with nothing more than a stroll through my house, but she gets crazed if she doesn't wear herself out every day."

"Gosh, yes. We have to figure this out, plus I've got new stuff to tell you from the phone calls I made today. I don't know if you could overhear anything from the back room—"

"Just the drunk guy who thought he'd entered a bar and was mad when you wouldn't serve him a martini."

"Oh, him. Terrence. He comes in a couple times a week."

"I bet he's only pretending to be drunk and secretly has a crush on you. But what about Clover?"

"Let's see if she'll be okay this evening with Tuffy's rainy day game. I call it the puppy Stairmaster. Where's her ball?"

I pulled it from my pocket and handed it over. Clover went on high alert. Janie led her to the top of the long stairway and gently rolled the ball off the top step. Clover watched intently as it bounced its way to the bottom, where it hit the closed door and ricocheted around the area between the door and the bottom step. She dashed down after it and brought it back to the top.

She dropped it by my foot and I nudged it over the edge once more. The next time when she dropped it, it rolled off on its own. I could see the light bulb go on over her head. We stood back and watched as she worked on perfecting her game, figuring out exactly how to drop the ball so that it would roll off.

"What do you think? Will that hold her for a while?"

"This is great. The stairs will wear her out and her brain is getting some exercise too."

"I'll take her and Tuffy out for a pee in a bit. Let's have some soup and I'll tell you what I've got in mind."

Steam rose in fragrant clouds from our bowls as we settled onto chairs at her teak dining table. The first sip was even better than I remembered from last night. Though possibly our near-death experience had honed my appreciation for simple pleasures.

Janie spread her napkin on her lap and picked up her spoon. "All right. It's obvious that you have not told me everything about this trouble you're in."

I started to speak, but she waved a hand at me. "That's okay, I get it. I mean we only met, what, two days ago? There is absolutely no reason you should trust me when everything else in your life has proved to be quicksand. Hopefully you'll realize I'm safe before I expire of curiosity—"

"I wish I could, but..."

"But what?"

"It could put you in—danger."

She gave me a long look. "I have to admit I'm not eager for that, the runaway car was beyond scary. But that's the thing. It could well be safer if we stick together."

"True."

"I don't have to know everything to see that the woman pretending to be you is up to her neck in this. So we need to get close to her."

"How? I don't know what she looks like or where she stays. If I go to the company and tell them I'm the real Beth, she'll have no trouble making me look like the liar. I have nothing left that will prove who I am. Not here, anyway, and North Carolina is a long way away."

"So be fake. Your disguise is good. Go in there as Mary Claire Johnson. She will never know it's you."

I thought about this. "You think I should, what, make an appointment with her? That would be surreal."

"Oh no." She paused to lift a spoonful of soup to her lips. "You're not going to visit her. You're going to work there and spy on her."

"What a good idea. And what sort of position am I to fill? Please say CEO. I've always wanted to be a CEO."

Her expression was nothing short of smug. She pointed her spoon at me. "Of course not, this is something much better. You had the good fortune to meet the exact right person at the dog park, the person who went to high school with the head of HR at a certain local corporation. You, Mary Claire Johnson, are the new mailroom clerk at Willamette Environmental. You start the day after tomorrow."

9

"Mailroom clerk is better than CEO?"

"For our purposes, much better. Think about it. Who wanders all through a company, going in and out of offices all day, yet no one pays them much attention? If the CEO walks in employees sit up straight and maintain eye contact. Mailroom person? Most people don't even say hello."

I could see her point. The possibilities were dazzling. My spoon clattered into the bowl. "I think you're onto something here."

"You bet I am. You're going to storm the castle— through the mouse hole. They'll never see you coming."

"But how did you get me a job, even this job, sight unseen? And what about the paperwork? They're going to want to see a Social Security card if nothing else."

"We're going to fudge our way through the paperwork. I told Valerie, my friend who works there, that you're my husband's cousin—"

"Ummm, husband?"

"He died four years ago. Cancer."

"I'm so sorry." I felt the stab of pain from my own loss yet again.

"Yeah, it sucked." Sadness flitted across her face. "But back to your new job. We have to make sure we have your story down so we both tell people the same thing. I said you were Bill's cousin, that you had decided to move here from Seattle, and I offered you a place to stay while you found a job. You've put all your belongings in storage and just brought a few things with you."

"This should all be easy to remember, being true except for the Seattle part."

"And your first day in town your purse was stolen."

"So I have no ID with me."

"Exactly. Valerie's always been a sucker for a hard luck story. That's why she has seven cats and a three-legged iguana. And she really did have an opening for a mailroom clerk. She feels bad that she can't offer you a full time job to start. It's only thirty hours a week. So no benefits, at least while you're on probation."

"That's probably good. Less paperwork."

"That's what I thought. We'll mess up one or two digits on your Social Security number, and I bet no one will notice. At least for a while."

"I'll just have to find out what's going on before that happens."

"Who knows, maybe we'll accidentally use a real person's number and they'll get credit for your work."

"And welcome to it. Janie, you really are brilliant."

She sketched a modest bow. "Thank you, thank you."

"Let me think a moment...okay, here's a problem. I have no idea what a Seattle accent sounds like."

"That's easy. You didn't grow up there. What's an easy one for you to do, that you won't accidentally slip out of?"

"Probably Boston. I—I went to college there."

"So you're originally from Boston, you've lived in Seattle the past ten years. Things weren't going well for you there, and Bill always told you what a great place Salem is. So here you are. What else?"

I thought for a moment. From the hallway I could hear Clover's ball thumping down the stairs yet again. I'd have to go take it away from her soon—

"Clover."

"What about her?"

"That's just it, what about her? I've only met a handful of people since I got here, but every single one of them has seen me with Clover."

"That's right. Damn."

"I don't know what the chances are that Mary Claire Johnson will run into Lisa and Darren, and if I did it probably wouldn't matter. But they must know I'd never go off and leave Clover."

"Maybe we could disguise her."

"How? If she had long hair we could give her a cut and that might do it, but she's so sleek she's practically a naked puppy already."

"True." Janie thought for a moment. "I know! We'll dye her. I saw this woman on TV who air brushes dye on dogs—"

"Oh yeah, like that poodle that they made look like a panda."

"Right! We can turn her from a dog with short white hair to a dog with short black hair. I even have an air brush. It was a donation that hasn't sold yet."

"I guess that might work..." I made a face.

"But you don't think so."

"I just don't know. I certainly would recognize her even if she's a different color. Maybe no one else would. But if it's not well done she might be even more conspicuous. Are you good with the air brush?"

"I've never used one."

"My gut instinct is to think of something else."

By now our bowls were empty. "Do you want more soup?" I asked. Janie shook her head, so I stood and gathered up the dishes. "Can I get you anything else?"

"There are still some brownies. Some chocolate would help us think."

"I should probably end Clover's session on the puppy Stairmaster. She still needs dinner."

"Yeah, Tuffy too. Let's feed the dogs and then I'll take them both out for their walkies. And then we will solve the Clover problem.

I let the fudgy goodness of the brownie linger on my tongue as I rocked back and forth in Janie's antique chair. She was back in her favorite spot on the sofa, with Tuffy snuggled beside her. Clover had settled at the other end, ready for a nap after her ball-chasing session. Janie gazed at her thoughtfully.

"How about putting her in a kennel? Just until you figure out what's going on?"

I grimaced. "Possible, I guess, but I really hate to do that. Unless you know of someplace with a stellar reputation, and even then I'm not sure I could do it. Plus there's the matter of paying for it. I *do* have money—or at least I did—but I have no way to access it."

"Let's ignore money for now and worry about it later. If nothing else you'll have a paycheck coming in from your mail clerk job."

"Which I suspect will not be a very large paycheck. I know I'm reacting emotionally, but Clover is about all I have at this point. Since I got her at the age of eight weeks we've never been apart for more than a few hours."

"Probably neither of you would do very well if we put her in a kennel. Okay, what about doggie day care? That way she'd at least get some exercise without our taking her to the dog park."

"But she'd still be here, signaling my presence."

"But other than the Banfields, who would she be signaling your presence to?"

"Whoever set me up. I could easily have been followed, probably from the apartment complex. From there it was the bank, the Banfields', the dog park, and you. Not a very long trail."

"True. But maybe we're getting too complicated here. I can put out the story that after your car burned, you needed to get back to North Carolina right away. Oh, wait. Did you tell Lisa and Darren about your job and apartment?"

I thought back to our conversations. "No. Just that the ATM ate my card, and the next day that the bank hadn't solved the problem but was working on it. I'm pretty sure that was it."

"So other than me, no one knows the true extent of your disaster?"

"You—and whoever caused it."

"Oh yeah, them. Let's put them aside for now. Starting tomorrow morning, I can tell anyone and everyone that because of your car disaster, you've gone back home. You've left Clover with me for a couple of weeks while you take care of business. I took you to PDX—"

"What's PDX?"

"The Portland airport. In fact I *will* take you to PDX tonight—"

"Janie, I have no identification. I couldn't even buy a ticket, let alone get on a plane."

"Who besides the two of us know that your purse burned up in the car?"

"Just the sheriff guy. I think."

"Good. Of course you're not going to fly, but the bad guys will think that you could. Besides saying you went back to North Carolina, I'll also say the timing worked out perfectly because Bill's cousin is arriving on the train from Seattle to stay with me for a few weeks. All you have to do is get from the airport to the Amtrak station and then actually take the train to Salem. It's the same train that leaves from Seattle. You'll take your Mary Claire disguise along and become her at the airport. Even if someone follows you that far, you can slip out unseen because they'll be watching for Beth, not Mary Claire, to come out of the bathroom."

"That could work. Do the trains run all night?"

"No, I don't think so, but I'll look them up in a minute. We can work that out. You may not get a lot of sleep tonight, but you can catch up tomorrow."

"Before I start my new job the day after."

"Yes. I know you'll want to be at your freshest for that."

"For sure." I took a deep breath. "All right, let's do it."

She jumped up from the sofa, spilling Tuffy off as well. Clover looked at them, then closed her eyes again.

That puppy Stairmaster was good.

"I'll start figuring out travel times," Janie announced and started for her computer.

"While you do that, may I borrow your phone?" She fished her cell out of her pocket and tossed it to me. I caught it one-handed. "I need to maintain my reputation as a polite Southerner."

"Hello?"

"Hi, Lisa? This is Beth Harding."

"Oh, hi, Beth! How's it going? Hey, I heard you had a car accident. Are you okay?"

"Yes, I'm fine. The car didn't make it, but Janie and the dogs and I are perfectly okay."

"That's good, I was worried. Though I feel terrible about your cute car. Did you get your bank thing straightened out?"

"They're still working on it. It has turned out to be complicated. Listen, I have to fly back home—"

"Gosh, really? I thought you'd come to Salem to stay."

"Oh, I'll be back. For my dog if nothing else. Janie has been kind enough to offer to keep her while I'm gone."

"That sounds just like her. She is always so nice."

What? Wait a minute, I thought, you don't really know her. You weren't even sure of her name. Aloud I said, "I know, she's great. And actually my trip works out perfectly for her. Her cousin, no, wait, maybe it's her husband's cousin, anyway, a cousin is coming down from Seattle. She's just found a job here and Janie offered her a place to stay while she looks around for her own place."

"Tell Janie I'll keep my ears open in case I hear of any good apartments opening up."

84

"I'll surely tell her. She's taking me up to PDX tonight—"

"Tonight! Wow, that's fast."

"I figured the quicker I go and get things settled, the quicker I can be back here to pick up Clover. But before I go, I just had to thank you for taking me in."

"It was nothing. I need to thank you for the lovely flowers."

"They were the least I could do. I'm sure I'll see you when I return, but I wanted to make sure you know I will never forget your kindness. And Darren's."

"Well, plan to stay with us again when you come back. You know we'll always be happy to see you."

"And maybe y'all will make it to North Carolina one of these days and stay with me."

"That's a promise."

We said our goodbyes, and I ended the call. Handing the phone back to Janie I said, "And now, let the games begin."

10

Valerie Frost was short, wide, and wearing the most beautiful skirted suit I had ever seen. Two-toned gray checks with a lavender silk blouse that set off her clear complexion and white curls perfectly. In contrast to her name, her smile was anything but frosty.

I handed her the large envelope of forms. "Thank you so much for giving me this chance to work here."

I had no trouble making that sound sincere.

"Well, it will be up to you to prove yourself, but I know you'll do just fine. I've never known Janie Morris to be wrong about a person and we go way, way back."

"That's what she said. I'll work very hard. I would never want to let her or you down."

She pulled sheets of paper from the envelope and glanced through them. "Very good, looks like everything is in order."

"It was nice of you to email the forms. I—I like to be able to make sure all the details are right on things like that."

Those forms were a work of art.

Valerie's expression became serious, and she leaned forward a bit in her chair. "Even though this is an entry level position, it is absolutely vital to the efficient functioning of the company. I don't know how much you know about Willamette Environmental Taskgroup. We are a leader in the field of environmental engineering, doing research and providing consultants to both government and private industry. Did you read over the list of duties that I included?"

"Oh, yes ma'am. In fact I've got the sheet in my pocket in case I need to refer to it."

Janie and I had giggled uncontrollably over that list and the earnest corporate-speak in which it was written. I learned that "the primary purpose and function of the mail room staff is to ensure the efficient flow of communications throughout the Taskgroup, providing quality customer service to internal customers." I must "live and exemplify the Five Precepts of Willamette Environmental within self and team: Probity, Responsibility, Congruity, Efficiency and Freedom." It went on to elaborate that we needed freedom to shape our destiny, and we needed profit to remain free. At that point Janie had begun singing "Born Free" in a high warbling soprano. I joined in until the dogs jumped on us and we collapsed under doggie kisses and wags.

Now, in Valerie's office, I studiously kept a straight face. "I'm ready to get started."

"Good girl. Let's take you down to the mail room. Andy Collins is the other mail room clerk and he's going to show you everything you need to know."

She led me out of her office and through a maze of corridors. I felt like I should be dropping breadcrumbs behind me for navigation. As we walked she pointed out various departments and features, including the staff lunch room which was called The Bistro on the duties list. "You probably noticed that you'll be keeping the machines in The Bistro filled. And of course that's where you can take breaks and lunch times."

We reached the end of a corridor where the hallway went around a corner. A few feet further on a woman stood waiting at the closed doors of an elevator.

"Oh, good, let me introduce you." Valerie led me to the other woman. "Mary, this is Beth. Mary is Andy's new assistant in the mailroom," she explained.

I froze like a mouse that has felt the shadow of the hawk pass over him.

"Oh, hi," said Beth, smiling at me and holding out her hand. "Beth Farjeon. I'm in accounting." I managed to shake hands, though my knees were weak with relief. "Welcome to WETCo. Are you two going up or down?"

"Oh, down," said Valerie. I saw that the up button was lit and reached out to push the other. A second later the bell dinged and the light on the Up button went out.

"Guess this is my ride," Beth said, stepping into the car. "Good luck with your new job, Mary Claire."

"Thanks." The elevator door closed, its vaguely shiny stainless steel face reflecting Valerie and me as two faceless shapes.

"The mail room is on the lowest level near the loading dock. This is the closest elevator, and there are two others in the building that access that floor as well."

The bell dinged again, and the down-button light went out. The door opened on an empty car, and we stepped in. Valerie pushed a button marked LL.

Lower Level. WETCo was evidently too classy to have a Basement.

"Can I get to the mailroom from the lobby?"

"No, if you come into the building through the lobby you'll have to go to one of the other elevators. The way this building is constructed on the side of a hill puts the lobby on what is actually the second floor. But you'll want to park in the lower lot and enter down there. Andy can show you."

Unlike the elevator I'd taken earlier from the lobby to the third floor, this one was a simple utilitarian metal box. Large enough to accommodate several people, or perhaps one mail room clerk and a large cart of mail. The ride was state of the art though; I hardly realized we had moved when the door opened on a new floor.

"Here we are." Valerie led me out of the elevator and toward a wide door that framed a brightly lit room crowded with bins, shelves and tables. As we entered I saw that modular desks topped with backless shelving had been arranged to enclose an area about ten feet wide and perhaps twice that long. The side of the shelving facing out had framed motivational posters hung at strategic intervals, making it hard to see into the enclosed area. Valerie led me toward the entry into the enclosure. I had to work hard to keep a straight face as I passed the poster showing an aircraft carrier steaming through calm waters with a flotilla of battleships in formation behind it.

The label was "Teamwork."

"Good morning, Andy!" Valerie called. I heard rustling in the enclosure, then a young man appeared.

"Hey, Valerie, what's up?"

"I've brought your new assistant. This is Mary."

"Umm, it's actually Mary Claire." I ducked my head in shy confusion.

"Oh yes, Mary Claire. And this is Andy Collins. Andy, you'll need to show Mary—sorry, Mary Claire— what to do. She hasn't worked in a mail room before but she comes highly recommended and I'm sure she'll learn everything in no time."

"I'll be happy to do that." Andy gave her a blinding smile. Valerie patted me once on the shoulder and left, her gray high heels clicking decisively on the tile floor.

Andy turned off the smile and studied me. I watched him covertly through the thick bangs of my wig, hoping it was still on straight. He seemed to be taking in every detail, and I was suddenly sure he was going to see right through my disguise and pronounce me a fraud.

He appeared to be in his mid-twenties, clean shaven, auburn hair brushed neatly from a side part. He had interesting taste in clothes. He wore crisp jeans, a long sleeved white shirt with the cuffs rolled up, and a V-neck cardigan vest that I was pretty sure was cashmere. The navy bow tie with gold metallic dots was the crowning touch.

"Jimmy Olsen." The words popped out of my mouth.

"What?"

"Oh, um, sorry. It's just—you look like Jimmy Olsen from the old Superman TV show. You know, the photographer who helped Clark Kent."

The dazzling smile returned. I could have sworn I saw a ray of light glinting from his teeth.

"That is *exactly* the effect I was going for. Brilliant. Mary Claire, come on in. We're going to get along just fine."

Andy's take on mail room work was simple. "They do not pay us enough. Period. I bet they're not even giving you any benefits."

I shook my head. "I'm part time. Thirty hours a week. Ten to four thirty. And a half-hour lunch."

"That figures. We don't even rate a full hour for lunch. We are the two lowest paid people in this building—"

"How do you know?"

"I hacked into the HR files. Even the security guy who wanders around the parking lot pretending to keep cars from being broken into makes more than we do. The receptionist in the lobby has us beat by five bucks an hour and all she does is look pretty and tell the guy from the florist where to put the new arrangement of flowers each week."

"Do they put them in different places?"

"No. It's always right in the center of the table that's directly between the front door and her desk."

"I had to walk around that table this morning."

"Of course you did. Well, the artful placement of that bouquet is thanks entirely to Gigi's labors. So after I'd been here a few weeks and figured out the lay of the land, I calculated how many hours a week at a fair wage WETCo is actually buying from me. And that's how many hours I work."

"Really? Do you just leave and no one notices?"

"I probably could, but mostly I enjoy my leisure, do some writing, sometimes do a little side business online. Now that you're here we'll be able to cover for each other. I think we're going to have a great time."

"I—I don't want to get into any trouble. I really need this job. I'm, uh, I've pretty much had to start my life over."

"Don't worry. I won't let anything happen to you. After all, it's not every day someone recognizes my Jimmy Olsen guise. You'll get the hang of this in no time. There's just one thing you have to remember."

"What's that?"

"If anyone, and I mean anyone, is in sight, look busy. Even if it's just Gigi the receptionist. Always have something with you to deliver, even if it's an empty envelope. Then when you're unobserved you can do what you want. Do you like to read?"

"I do. I love to read." I nodded enthusiastically.

"Then welcome to WETCo."

"So there's, like, no security cameras or anything? They're not spying on us?"

"There are a few cameras in select locations, and you want to use those strategically."

"How do I do that?"

"That's your chance to really hustle. The hallway with a camera is the one you pass through with your most purposeful walk. You never stop there for a conversation, just nod to anyone you pass and keep going."

"When Mrs. Frost—"

"You can call her Valerie. We're relentlessly on a first name basis here."

"Okay. Valerie. When she was bringing me down here, every corridor looked alike. How do I know which ones have cameras?"

"You'll learn the layout in no time. The building is basically a big square with a main hallway on each floor. On one side of the corridor are the outer offices that have windows, and on the other side are the inner offices. Some sections have multiple rooms, and just one or two doors onto the hallway."

"Are the cameras visible?"

"Oh yeah. They'd never spend the money on hiding them."

"This all sounds a lot like high school."

"Totally. Just make sure you look industrious when someone can see you, and the rest of the time you can safely embrace your slacker side."

"Why are you telling me all this? You don't know if you can trust me."

"Yes I do. I know everything about you I need to know."

"How?"

"Mary Claire, you saw right through me to my inner Jimmy Olsen. That's good enough for me."

Janie and Clover both pounced on me the minute I walked into the thrift store that afternoon. Clover's tail thrashed wildly as she uttered little crooning noises. Janie grabbed my arm and demanded, "Well? Did you see her?"

"No, not yet," I said to Janie, and to Clover, "Baby girl! Did you miss me?" I looked around the thrift store. Two teenage girls were going through a rack of sweaters, and back in the housewares a balding middle aged man was holding a wine glass up to the light. "We should wait until we're alone to talk. Want me to go work in the back room till you close?"

"Heck no. The first day of a new job is exhausting. Go put your feet up. And if you don't mind, turn the oven on to three fifty at, oh, six fifteen, and about ten minutes later pop in the casserole that's in the fridge."

"You bet. My feet are tired but this is not going to be exhausting work. I'll tell you everything over dinner. But first I'll take the dogs out before I climb that Mt. Everest of stairs."

We sat down to eat at about seven. I took a sip of wine, then tasted the casserole. Delicious. After only a few days I felt so at home. My shoulders eased down a notch.

"Was Valerie wearing one of her fabulous suits?" Janie wanted to know. I could tell she was easing me into the topic of my day at Willamette Environmental.

"She was. Is she famous for them? With a silk blouse and wonderful sh—"

She threw her napkin at me. "Okay, okay, tell me the good stuff."

"My paperwork passed muster. She took me down to the mailroom after a few minutes, where I met Andy."

"Andy who?"

"Collins. He's—"

She lit up like a fireworks display. "Andy Collins! I know him. He's terrific."

"You're sure it's the same one? Mid-twenties, reddish hair, snappy dresser?"

"That's Andy. I did some community theater a few years ago and Andy was involved. You're going to love him. He's about ten years older than my son Jasper, and he was always really nice to him."

"He certainly was nice to me. So today he showed me how to get packages into the mail, and open and sort the incoming stuff. We did one delivery round together with him introducing me to people. Like you said, most of them barely looked up."

"So what about the fake Beth?"

"I didn't want to show obvious interest in her. I mean, there's no way Mary Claire could even have heard of her, right? I have to tell you, it was very weird to see a mail slot with my name on it."

"I bet."

"If and when some mail comes in addressed to Beth Harding it's going to be very hard not to read it."

"Legally I suppose you could."

"I wouldn't want to take it to court. Anyway, I can tell from the row her mail slot is in that her office is on the top floor. Which is the only floor with any security."

"I thought they hired you to do research. Why would a researcher need to be on a secure floor?"

I bit my lip. I should have been more careful in what I told her.

"Beth? Come on, why is the fake Beth on a secure floor?"

"I can't tell you."

"Tell me!"

"I can't. Really."

"Tell me something, or I'll...I'll..."

I had to laugh at her attempt to find a dire enough threat. "You'll what?"

"I'll hide Clover's favorite ball. That'll show you."

"Obviously I cannot let you punish my dog."

"You give me no choice." She tried to keep her expression stern, but I could see she was holding back a smile. I was serious when I replied.

"Janie, I told you, it isn't safe for you to know anything."

"Safe or not. Tell me."

I struggled with what to say, and finally came out with, "I, well we, my sister and I, we invented something. It needs more testing before it can be brought to the market. I made a deal with Willamette Environmental to do that, as well as the manufacturing and marketing."

"Wow. I don't think I ever knew an inventor." She thought for a moment. "But Beth, what did you invent that could be dangerous for me to know about?"

I shook my head. "No. I really can't tell you."

"It's not a—a weapon is it?"

"No, nothing like that."

"All right, we'll leave it for now. But one of these days you're going to have to tell me."

"As soon as I can, I will. Just let me find out what's going on, and all my secrets will be yours."

"So you need to get access to the secure floor and the fake Beth."

"Yes. Several people on that floor did have mail today, so Andy took me up there to deliver it. But I never even saw an office with my name on it, let alone the person occupying it. I couldn't think of any reason to wander around looking for her."

"I suppose that might have looked odd. Even to Andy, and he takes everything in stride."

"Until she gets some mail, I'm not sure what to do."

Janie brightened. "What a good idea!"

"What?"

"We'll send her some mail."

11

Getting the envelope addressed to Beth Harding into the incoming mail was a piece of cake. I slid it into the bunch in my hand, and when I came to it as I sorted mail into slots, I held it up.

"Andy, this one says 'Personal' on it. Do I do anything different with it?"

"Nah, just stick it in the slot. Who's it for?"

I looked at the envelope. "Someone called Beth Harding."

"Oh. Her." A flat note in his voice sent a tingle over my scalp.

"What?"

"It's nothing."

"No, tell me."

He grimaced. "Maybe I'm being unfair. She only started working here a couple of weeks ago."

"Has she done something to you?"

"It's more her attitude. I mean, a lot of people ignore you if you're the lackey from the mail room, it doesn't usually bother me. I can't really put my finger on it. Every time I see her I find I'm gritting my teeth."

I knew I liked this guy.

"Did we see her yesterday?"

He thought for a moment. "No, I don't think so. You'd remember her because she's got this Southern accent, she's from Georgia or Alabama or someplace like that."

"That's a long way from Oregon." In so many ways, I thought. "What does she do? For the company, I mean."

"They hired her to head up some project. No one seems to know what it is." He grabbed a handful of mail and began firing it into slots, ten times faster than me. Of course he had the advantage of knowing where each person's mail slot was located. "There was a lot of buzz before she got here. I heard she's super smart. Maybe that's what makes her think she's a cut above the rest of us."

"Really smart people know better than to show off how smart they are."

He laughed. "That's probably true. Whatever the project is that she's working on, the big cheeses think it's going to make a whole lot of money."

"Every company wants that."

"Of course they do. Though companies differ in what they're willing to do to make a lot of money."

"So do people."

Before long the morning mail delivery was sorted.
"Tell you what," Andy said, "one of us can start on the
bottom floor and the other on the top. We'll meet
somewhere in the middle. Then we can go make sure
the machines are full enough that no one will riot over
the last Gooshy Bar, and then we can come back here
and hide."

"What in the world is a Gooshy Bar?"

"Local candy bar. The full name is Ooshy Gooshy
Bar."

"Sounds awful."

"The name may be awful but the candy is good.
There's practically a cult following here." His eyes lit
up at some memory. "That woman you were asking me
about earlier—"

"Beth Harding?"

"Right. She hits the machine every day at three
o'clock for a Gooshy bar. She got there right after Tom
Redmond snagged the last one the other day and I
thought she was going to deck him."

"Must be some candy bar."

"She sure thinks so. If she'd been nice Tom would
probably have given it to her. He's a good guy. But she
was so nasty that he ate it right in front of her."

"Thanks for the warning. I'll try not to get
between her and any Gooshy bars."

"Good plan. So, do you want to start at the bottom
or the top?"

I grinned at him. "The top, definitely. This may be the only time in my life I get to start at the top."

The rubber wheels of my mail cart whispered along the carpeted corridor. My heartbeat quickened. My quarry was near. I kept my pace deliberate, stepping into offices and placing mail in inboxes. A few people had letters or packages ready to go out; I added those to the cart. One or two said hello or good morning.

It was easy to keep my head down. Mary Claire needed a reputation as being very shy.

I kept the letter addressed to Beth Harding, in care of the company and marked "Personal," until last, partly through reluctance to be in the presence of the person who had taken so much from me, and partly because I had some idea I might need to make a quick getaway.

I found the door with my name on a blue card slotted into a holder by the jamb. The door was closed, but the latch had not caught. I listened for a moment and heard nothing from within. Keeping my breathing as even as I could, I gave two tentative knocks on the door. Waited. Tapped again, a little harder. The door inched open. I strained to hear the sound of computer keys clacking or papers rustling, but there was nothing. I bit my lip. She could be in there sitting silently, thinking. Plotting.

I tapped once more, and when there was still no response I pushed the door open wide enough to peek in.

She wasn't in her office. My office. The desk I had expected to occupy was untenanted, the chair pushed back and turned slightly toward the windows.

Morning light flooded the room. The outer wall had a built-in credenza that stretched the full width of the room; above it glass rose to the ceiling. Pinch pleated draperies in a subdued print brought a little color into the otherwise beige space. The credenza had two locking sections, probably lateral file drawers, and two pairs of cabinet doors without locks.

On the left wall, opposite the desk, a door to another lighted room was slightly open. I had been promised a workroom as well as an office in my contract with Willamette Environmental; that must be the space. I jumped when a voice suddenly spoke from that direction.

"No! I told you that...then you shouldn't have let them get away..."

It sounded like a phone conversation. And if this was indeed the imposter, she was not using her fake accent.

"I can't possibly finish by then..." A long pause, then, "How the hell would I know that? If you think—"

My self-preservation instincts kicked in. I dropped the letter in the middle of the blotter on the desk and turned toward the door. *Get out, get out now* was all I could think. I was almost to the door when a sharp voice behind me said, "Hey! What are you doing in here?"

I drew in a steadying breath and half turned, keeping my face lowered. "I—I brought you a letter. On your desk."

She stood in the doorway of the adjoining room, cell phone still held to her ear. Into this she said, "Hold on, someone's here." She barely flicked a glance at me. "You're from the mail room? Take that box there by the door and make sure it goes out today. Oh, and that plate on my desk needs to go back to the lunchroom."

I noticed she didn't remember to use the accent when she spoke to me. Or felt she didn't need to bother.

She turned back into the adjoining room as she returned the phone to her ear. "I'm here...Oh, just some woman delivering mail..." The door closed behind her.

I added the package to my cart, then picked up the plate on her desk. Something red was dried on its surface, tomato sauce perhaps.

On the way back to the elevator I stepped into the ladies room. Looking around to make sure I was unobserved, I shoved the plate deep into the trash bin.

Over fragrant plates of pad si-ew and panang curry at Janie's favorite Thai restaurant that evening, I filled her in on my day.

"It's not much, but I can tell you two things about her for sure." I sipped some of the rich yellow broth from the curry. "She did not recognize me—"

"I knew she wouldn't." Janie speared one of her wide noodles. "Your Mary Claire disguise is good."

"Yes, and thank you very much for Mary Claire. The other thing is, she wasn't using her accent for whoever she was talking to on the phone."

"Interesting. So she probably wasn't talking to a coworker. Wait, did she put it back on when she talked to you?"

"Nope. She only said about three sentences to me, but I would have noticed. She either forgot, or didn't think I was worth the bother."

"Good. We want her to think that the mail room clerk is a nobody who knows nothing and wouldn't say boo to a banana." She went after a piece of broccoli on her plate, then said, "We also know she's a complete and total rip-roaring bitch. That bit with the plate..." She shook her head and gave a little snort. "I'd have thrown it away in *her* trash can, and I wouldn't have covered it up, either."

"It was tempting." I sipped my Thai iced tea. "There's something else, though. I only saw her for a few seconds, but my first thought was that there was something familiar about her. I've seen her some place before."

"Really? You can't remember where?"

I shook my head. "No, I've been wracking my brain. It's like when you have a word on the tip of your tongue but you just can't say it."

"Maybe she was following you for a while before she took over your life. You might have spotted her, you know, peripherally."

"Maybe. In fact that seems likely. I'd certainly want to know all I could about a person before I tried to impersonate them."

"No, wait a minute. She doesn't have to pretend to act like you. You came to a new place where no one knows you. Even what you look like. As long as it was a woman roughly your age with a Southern accent, she could do or be anything. She doesn't have to copy your walk, your mannerisms, anything."

"You're depressing me."

"I'm depressing myself," she admitted. "We're just going to have to find out more about her."

"How? Any information I find at Willamette Environmental would just be my own information."

"So we need to find out who she really is. And who she's working with. I'm convinced she's not doing this alone."

"I don't know." I thought for a moment about the phone call I had overheard. "I think she could be working alone, but—it does feel bigger than that. It's possible she was talking to a confederate when I overheard her today. It sounded like someone was pushing her about something. She certainly sounded annoyed."

"Okay, here's something I'm wondering about: whoever she is, how likely is it that she could fake your skills? I mean, whatever they hired you to do—"

"Janie..." I put a warning note in my voice.

"I know, I know, it's not safe for you to tell me. Yet. But whatever it is, will she actually be able to do what you can do?"

106

"No."

"No. No question about it?"

"None."

"That's what I thought. So, how long will it be before someone at Willamette Environmental notices that she's not performing? Basically before she gets fired?"

"Mmmm. Good question. When we were interviewing I gave them an estimated minimum timeline of six weeks to three months, but maybe longer, to solve the piece I've been working on—"

"Piece of what?"

"Can't tell you."

"I thought maybe I could just slide it in there and you wouldn't notice. Go on."

"I was expecting to work with other people, so I would have spent the first couple of weeks getting them on board. No, do not ask me on board for what."

"I wasn't going to. Okay, yes, I was, but I actually do have another question."

"Yes?"

"The woman pretending to be you and probably one or more cohorts have stolen everything from you. They have all your computer passwords. They have shut you out of all your financial accounts. They took your moving van away with your personal belongings and cancelled your lease."

"You're depressing me again."

"Here's what I don't get. Why is she bothering to work there, pretending to be you? Why risk possible exposure, since she can't actually do your work? Why not just abscond with all your worldly goods and chattels and be done with it?"

I spooned up some rice and curry sauce and chewed. Took a sip of tea. Sighed. "Because what they're after is really big. And they don't have everything. Yet."

12

The next afternoon I stuck the last postage label on the last package and tossed it into the outgoing bin. The company van was parked at the loading dock just outside the mail room.

"That's it for today," I said. "Want me help you load these onto the van?"

Andy threw open the van's side door. "Sure. And then you're free as a bird for the rest of the day while I will be toiling away, waiting in line at the P.O."

"Birds work hard to survive," I pointed out.

"True," he countered, "but they get to fly."

The outgoing mail was light today and in a few minutes he drove away. I walked the few feet to where I had parked Janie's son's car. She had insisted that I borrow it to drive to work.

"I promised him I'd drive it regularly while he's at school. So you're doing me a favor."

"Sure I am. Like I'm doing you a favor staying in Jasper's room and eating you out of house and home. And allowing you to walk my dog."

She opened her eyes wider. "That's true! My gosh, little did I know what an altruist you'd turn out to be. But seriously, you need to get back and forth to work and his car is just sitting there."

"My driver's license got burned up in my car, remember? I should take the bus."

"Take the damned car. You might need it to follow someone. Just don't do anything to get stopped by the cops."

And so here I was in Jasper's car, waiting to follow someone.

Willamette Environmental had two parking lots. The larger was accessed down a sloping drive that led behind the building; a pretty little creek bordered the far side. The smaller lot lay between the building and the street, and had just enough spaces for a few visitors and a handful of the higher ranking employees of the firm.

I did a quick cruise through the lower lot, scanning for any out-of-state license plates. There were a couple from Washington, one from California, and one from Idaho; the rest were all Oregon.

I was betting that someone who would tell the mail room clerk to return a dirty plate would feel entitled to park in the upper lot. So I headed up the drive and did the same scan in the upper lot.

110

Every car had an Oregon plate.

Whoever I was up against did not carry their attention to detail to the extent of providing the fake Beth Harding with an appropriate car. But if anyone noticed, she could simply say she'd rented or borrowed a car, or flown here and bought one when she arrived.

A white SUV turned in from the street and drove up to the front of the building. In a couple of minutes, a man in his late thirties hurried out and opened the passenger door. I saw two small children bouncing up and down in the back seat. "Daddy! Daddy!" floated across the parking lot.

Maybe Fake Beth didn't have a car. Someone could give her a ride every day.

I couldn't wait in the upper lot. Even this late in the day, the only open parking spaces were marked Visitor, and they were too conspicuous. I scanned my surroundings. There were thick hedges separating the Willamette Environmental campus from the building next door. But directly across the street was another larger parking lot surrounding a five-story office building. The parking spaces furthest from their front door faced the driveway I wanted to watch, and there were several empty slots. I guided Jasper's car across the street and parked.

And waited.

Earlier in the day, I had timed a visit to The Bistro (wanting to roll my eyes as I always did when I saw the name) to coincide with Fake Beth's daily trek to the candy machine. Andy had been right; at about two minutes after three she came in, put a dollar bill in the machine, and punched the number for an Ooshy Gooshy bar. She left immediately with her treasure. She never noticed I was in the room, just a few feet away. I gave her very low points for her observational skills.

But now I knew what she was wearing, black slacks, black silk blouse. And I'd gotten a better look at her face.

After a bit, WETCo employees began leaving for the day. At first it was easy to see who was driving every car, and who exited from the front door. Andy returned in the van and guided it down the hill and out of sight around the building. By five o'clock there was a steady stream of my coworkers heading home.

Which is when I realized that wearing black was practically a dress code. From black jeans and black sweatshirts to black suits with crisp shirts in white or blue, Willamette Environmental folks loved their black.

People were leaving in packs now, waiting in line to turn their cars onto the street and homeward. A few rode motorcycles, and I was completely unsurprised to see they were covered with black riding gear and helmets with smoky face guards.

"Don't panic," I commanded out loud. "If you don't follow her today you can try again tomorrow."

Someone knocked on my passenger side window and I let out a scream. Andy stood grinning beside the car. Wearing a black jacket and holding a black motorcycle helmet. I turned the key in the ignition so I could roll down the window, my heart still pounding.

"Do not ever, I mean ever, pound on a woman's car window. It scares the crap out of us."

His eyebrows rose in chagrin. "I'm sorry, Mary Claire, I didn't think. What the heck are you doing here?"

"I—" My mind was blank. "I, uh, needed to think about something before I go home."

"But why are you driving Jasper Morris's car?"

"What makes you think this is Jasper Morris's car?"

"Right make, model, color, dent on passenger door and bumper sticker that says 'Bigfoot saw me and no one believes him.'"

Damn. Did this guy miss anything? "He's at college. His mom lent me his car." I realized several cars had left the WETCo parking lot and I hadn't seen who was driving.

"But why—"

"Oh hell. Get in." I unlocked the passenger door. He climbed in, holding the helmet on his lap, and turned to me. I tried to watch for my quarry without appearing to.

"So why would Janie lend you Jasper's car? Though come to think of it, it's exactly the kind of thing she would do."

I retrieved our Mary Claire cover story from the back of my mind. "We're related. Her husband was my cousin."

"I see. Bill was a great guy."

I thought of my sister, and brought that loss into my voice. "Yeah. Very much missed."

113

We sat in silence for a minute. I watched the building across the street. I could feel Andy's eyes on me. The stream of cars leaving Willamette Environmental was slowing. Still no sign of Fake Beth. At last I glanced at him.

"What do you want, Andy?"

"I want to know what you're doing here."

"I told you, I need a few minutes to think before I go home. Well, back to Janie's place. I'm staying with her for now."

"Uh huh. You needed to think."

I looked at him more fully. "Yes, I needed to think. Anything wrong with that?"

"The parking lot across the street from WETCo seems an odd place for you to do your thinking."

"I started to leave and then changed my mind and pulled in here."

"Uh huh. And does your thinking have anything to do with the way you're watching everyone leaving our building?"

"I—I'm not. I was just—just looking in that direction."

He gave me a big friendly grin. "Oh, go on. You were not."

"Was too."

"Were not."

I couldn't help it. I laughed. "Suddenly I feel about four years old."

He began to hum the song "Young at Heart" in a surprisingly mellow voice. Then he said, "Okay, you're just sitting here thinking. But if you *did* happen to be watching our fellow wage slaves leaving WETCo—"

"I'm not."

He ignored me. "—and if you were actually looking for a particular person—"

"No. Really."

"—and if that person might just possibly be the recently hired, bad-tempered Southern belle going by the name of Beth Harding—"

I caught my breath.

"—then she is about to leave the parking lot in her black BMW."

13

"What? No."

He pointed. And there she was, in a shiny, late-model BMW sedan, waiting for a car on the street to pass so she could go. Her left turn signal was flashing.

"Damn," I muttered. I turned on Andy. "Get out. I've got to leave."

"Nope."

"Get out."

"I'm coming with you."

I started the engine and pointed at the passenger door. "Out."

"You'd better drive. She's going to get away."

I put the car in reverse and backed around his motorcycle. "Go. I mean it."

"I'll be helpful. You drive and I'll keep an eye on her."

From the corner of my eye I saw that the traffic had cleared and the BMW was moving. I gave up on Andy and threw Jasper's car into gear. In a few seconds we were turning onto the street in the same direction the BMW was headed, a couple of cars between us. A block ahead was a stop sign at a T intersection.

"She's got her right blinker on," Andy informed me.

Only one of the cars between us turned right. "I hope she doesn't spot us."

"I don't think she will, and even if she does we're just fellow employees leaving work for the day. She probably wouldn't recognize us even if she sees us, since we're just the peons from the mail room."

"That's true. She does have a nose-in-the-air quality."

"Okay, she's turning again—"

"I can see her. She's only one car away."

"Sorry, just trying to be helpful. I wonder if she lives in this neighborhood."

Fake Beth's right turn took her onto a residential street. In a moment I followed her. "I don't like this. We're too conspicuous now."

"No turnoffs for about three blocks on this street. Pull over in front of a house so it looks like we're home, and we'll see where she goes."

I did as he said and we waited, both of us focused on the BMW getting smaller in the distance. In a moment he said, "Wait for it...okay, she's not turning.

Let's go. She'll be at Commercial in a moment and we want to see which direction she takes."

I pulled away from the curb, going about ten miles over the twenty-five mile per hour speed limit. I mentally crossed my fingers that I wouldn't get pulled over, having no idea how I would try to talk my way out of showing a driver's license that had been reduced to ash in a Christmas tree field. But the BMW was held up by heavy traffic on the main drag, and once I was only a block away I slowed down. Then the black sedan turned right. A few seconds later we followed.

"I wonder who showed her the shortcut through that neighborhood," Andy commented.

"Maybe she lives there. Maybe she has to go pick up her kids. Maybe—"

"Maybe she's lived around here all her life and knows Salem like the back of her hand."

I shot him a look. "You said she's from the South."

"*She* says she's from the South. Big difference. I'd guess if she's southern anything it's probably southern California."

The traffic light ahead changed to yellow, and the car in front of the BMW slowed and stopped, forcing her to do the same. "But what about her accent?"

"Oh, puh-lease," he drawled. "That accent could have come out of a Cracker Jack box. Haven't you noticed how it keeps slipping?"

"I've only seen her twice." I decided not to mention that she'd forgotten the accent completely when I'd delivered the mail to her office.

"Her Southern accent is more wayward than Olympia Dukakis's was in *Steel Magnolias.*"

I struggled to keep a straight face. I loved Olympia, but I knew exactly what he meant. The light changed and we started up again. In a few blocks the road curved to the right and we were on Liberty Street in the one-way section of town.

"I wonder if she's going downtown, or maybe taking the Parkway to the freeway. How's your gas?"

I glanced down at the gauge. "We're good."

"There's a car signaling ahead to leave a parking place," he warned me. "Okay, the Beemer's got its signal on, she's going to park."

He reached for the door handle as our lane of traffic slowed. "I'll jump out here and keep an eye on her. Park the car and come find me. I'll try to stay in sight, or at least keep watching for you." He pointed to a building ahead. "There's a slightly hidden parking lot back there, might have a space this time of day."

I touched the brakes and he hopped out, leaving the bulky helmet on the passenger seat. I watched him stroll away, stopping to peer in the window of a shoe store. No one could have discerned that his attention was fixed on the black sedan that had just parked a few feet ahead of him.

Behind me a horn sounded, and I realized the cars in front of me were moving. I put on my turn signal to go around the corner and look for the slightly hidden parking lot.

Andy was right; there were several empty spaces in the lot. Most of the small businesses it bordered had closed at five o'clock, and the tiny coffee shop that was still open had a deserted air. I pulled into a slot, turned off the car, and unlocked my seatbelt. I reached for the door handle, then paused.

What was I doing letting Andy into the debacle my life had become? And why was he so insistent...and so observant? But how could I have stopped him? I might have been able to shove him out of the car, but it would have made for a very awkward atmosphere in the mail room tomorrow.

On the other hand, I was not at all sure what kind of atmosphere would exist there after this afternoon's adventure.

I scratched surreptitiously under the wig, then looked into the rear view mirror to make sure the thing was still straight and looked at least somewhat authentic. The eyes that looked back at me were shadowed and tired.

"Buck up." I spoke a little too loudly. "You're going to get through this. And as long as you still have Clover, that's all that really matters."

I found Andy sitting at a sidewalk table with a mug of steaming coffee in front of him. A second chair was pulled up by a tall glass of iced tea.

"Did I remember correctly that's your beverage of choice?"

"Thanks, it's great. I like the smell of coffee but not the taste."

He shook his head pityingly. "You poor thing."

I sat down and looked around. No Fake Beth in sight. "Did you lose her?"

"Of course not. She's in there—" he gave a slight jerk of his head— "having a drink with some guy. No, don't turn around. I've got them in sight."

"I wish I could hear them, but I suppose that would be pushing things."

"I doubt she's ever paid enough attention to either of us to recognize us in an unfamiliar location. Probably not even at WETCo. When I went in for our drinks, their tone was somewhat flirtatious, but I didn't hear much actual conversation."

"I wonder how long they'll be. I—I was hoping to follow her home. There's a reason I need to know where she lives."

He gave me an exasperated look. "Is that all? Mary Claire, why didn't you say so?"

"When did I have a chance to?" I took a deep breath. "And why are you butting in like this anyway? I distinctly remember telling you to get out of the car."

"Funny, I don't think I heard you say that. *I* distinctly remember you saying something like come on, it will be fun to follow an annoying coworker through evening rush hour traffic."

He seemed always to be making me laugh. "Gosh, you're right, that's exactly what I said. How could I have forgotten so soon?"

"We'll have to work on your long term memory skills. Meanwhile, do you actually need to see where she lives, or would her address be enough?"

"You know her address?"

121

"Not off hand. But you must not have been paying attention during your orientation in the mail room your first morning."

"What do you mean?"

"I told you, I can hack into the HR files. Unless she told a fib on her employment paperwork, we just have to look there for her address."

"Maybe we'd better keep following her."

"You mean—"

"Yes. I have reason to think there might be one or two small inaccuracies in her paperwork."

He started to say something, then focused on the other side of the window we were sitting by. "Don't look now, but I think they're coming out."

We kept our faces lowered as Fake Beth left the coffee shop. I risked a quick look as she said goodbye to her companion, catching them in a long kiss. His back was to us; her eyes were closed. When they broke apart, he walked up the street away from us. Fake Beth passed our table without a glance and strolled down the street to her car. As soon as she was far enough away, Andy stood.

"You coming?"

His voice seemed far away. I stood and looked down the street at the man walking quickly away. The plaid of his Pendleton shirt looked familiar, though I knew there must be a lot of Pendletons around.

But from the back, he looked very much like Darren Banfield.

14

By the time we got back to the car and out of the parking lot, the black BMW had disappeared.

"Don't worry," Andy said, "by this time tomorrow you'll know everything about her that HR knows."

The next day we rushed through the usual morning duties. Mail was sorted and delivered, copy machine toner replaced, outgoing packages prepped, and a joking conversation was carried on with the UPS guy. We helped set up a conference room for a meeting. Andy called a local garage to schedule maintenance for the company's van. And the candy machine in The Bistro was restocked with all its usual contents, including a new supply of Ooshy Gooshy Bars. Then Andy settled in at the mail room computer while I kept watch from behind the sorting shelves that shielded us from the open door into the hallway.

Hacking into the HR files didn't take long. I wondered how often Andy did it, or whether Willamette Environmental's security on its files was particularly lax. Whatever the reason, after a few minutes at the keyboard, Andy pushed his chair away and stood, gesturing toward the seat.

"Voilà, all yours. Looks like Valerie has scanned everything into the file. She's very efficient."

"Thanks." I settled on the chair and rolled close to the desk to look over the document on the screen, headed "Willamette Environmental Taskgroup Basic Employee Information."

"This looks useful," I commented. I studied the document.

The first section included the usual contact information, name, address, phone numbers, birth date, Social Security number. I saw that the birth date given was my real one, as was the SSN. I made a note of the address and phone numbers, including the office number and her cell.

"Do you know where this address is?" I asked Andy. He peered over my shoulder at the screen.

"Hmmm, let me think. I'm not familiar with the street. That zip code is South Salem but that hardly narrows it down. Here, put it into Google Maps."

He grabbed the mouse and in a few clicks had the map program on the screen. I typed in the address, and clicked the search button.

"Okay, got it. Just off Skyline and Croisan Scenic. Look, there's a street named Anaconda. Who would want to live on Anaconda Street?"

"Another anaconda? What kind of neighborhood is it? Aside from the resident anacondas."

"Ummm, probably houses from the Eighties, maybe Nineties. Mostly single-family homes, some apartment complexes. Here, click on the street view."

Footsteps sounded from the hall and someone called, "Hello?"

"Be right there!" Andy called back, and hurried to take care of whoever it was. I dimly registered their conversation about an expected special delivery package and how it was to be signed for as I studied the image on the screen. The Google van had passed by early on a sunny morning, so there were long shadows falling across the sidewalks onto the street. The street appeared to rise uphill for a couple of blocks, then leveled out. The houses were all painted in earth tones and had clearly been built in the same time period. I looked closely at the one matching the address on the employment form, a one-story ranch style clad in beige stucco. Other than the house number, nothing about it stood out from its neighbors.

I clicked back on the employment form and quickly scanned the rest of it. The next section was for job information—position, supervisor and so on— followed by emergency contact information. I made notes of that information, but expected all of it would be false.

Andy was back. "Got him sorted. How are you doing?"

"Okay, I've made a few notes. What else is in the file?"

He pointed to the file icon and I clicked. A long list of documents. I clicked on the one labeled Direct Deposit form. It was headed with my real name, the Fake Beth's address and phone, and then had information filled in for a local bank. At the bottom of the scanned sheet was an image of a very plain check, the kind you receive when you open a new account, with VOID printed across it in careful block letters.

I copied the sheet and pasted the information into a Word document. If and when I got my life back, I wanted to be able to access this account and the salary I should have been earning.

I couldn't help feeling I'd more than earned it even if I wasn't upstairs occupying that office and workroom, perfecting the project that had brought me to Oregon. And I hoped that this account would lead me to wherever they had stashed what had been taken from the accounts Fake Beth had closed.

One of the boxes that had been loaded onto the moving van had been labeled "Financial Documents." Stupid me. The box of checks in there had made it easy for her to impersonate me at the bank. I made a vow to use code words or ciphers to label boxes should I ever move again—and have accumulated enough possessions to require the assistance of movers. No need to make it quite so easy to be hijacked.

After work that afternoon I drove straight to the address on the Fake Beth's forms. A couple of doors down from her house I noticed a For Sale sign in a front yard, and drove by slowly. That house was clearly empty, so I did a U turn and cruised back to it. I parked in front and got my Kindle out for camouflage. If anyone asked what I was doing, I would say I was waiting for my real estate agent. There were two agents' names on the sign. I figured I could use either one. I'd keep my fingers crossed that I wouldn't somehow pick the name of someone who'd been killed a few days earlier in a tragic accident that everyone in town knew about except me.

I waited. Behind me the sun got lower and the shadows longer, and a note of chill crept into the air. The street was deserted until an SUV driven by a teenage girl parked in a drive up the street. Fifteen minutes later a large gray striped cat trotted across the street carrying a crisp dried leaf and disappeared under a bush.

I waited. And thought. I'd known when I decided to take the job with Willamette Environmental Taskgroup that the project I was bringing them for final development had the potential to be...well, world-changing. I'd told myself the potential for doing good outweighed the possible dangers. Even if ultimately the project failed, I had to try.

I had not had the foresight or the imagination to expect the attack that had been made upon my life.

I waited. A black car came up the street, but it wasn't a BMW and it rolled into the garage of a house behind me. The place I was watching remained dark and still. Fake Beth seemed to be one of those people who did not go straight home from work.

The cheap disposable phone in my pocket rang, making me jump. Only Janie and Willamette Environmental had the number, and it had never rung before. I fished it out and flipped it open, wondering why Janie was calling. "Hello?"

But it wasn't Janie.

"Mary Claire? It's Andy."

Of course it was. He would have taken a look at my employment file as soon as he could, and it included the number of this cheapo phone. The other ninety-eight percent of what he read was pure fiction.

"Andy? What's up?"

"Are you by any chance watching the house at the address in Beth Harding's file?"

A little chill trickled down my back. "Ummm...why do you ask?"

"Come on, are you?"

"Okay, yes. But she hasn't come home. I was about to give up."

"I thought that's where you would be." He sounded positively gleeful. "I think she gave a fake address on her forms."

"What do you mean?"

"I'm pretty sure she lives somewhere else. I followed her after work—"

"Andy!"

"—and she went straight to a townhouse on Madrona, let herself in, and then came out again in

128

fifteen minutes wearing different clothes. She got back in her car and drove off. I followed until she got on the freeway going north."

"So she's probably on her way to Portland."

"That's what I figured. Or maybe a shopping spree at the outlets in Woodburn. I decided to ditch the chase for tonight. Hope that's okay."

"Of course. I can't believe you did that much."

"Actually, it was fun. A bike is perfect for following someone."

"And you have that nice all-concealing helmet to keep anyone from recognizing you."

"Right. Anyway, you can stop camping out at that other house. I don't think she's living there."

"I'm sure you're right. What made you decide to follow her?"

"I figured you would check it out when you got off work. And that woman is as fake as a three dollar bill. I was betting that her paperwork was too."

"At least I can go home now."

"Do you want the address of the townhouse?"

"I don't need it tonight. You can give it to me at work tomorrow."

"Okay. See you in the morning."

"'Bye. And—thanks, Andy."

I ended the call and sat holding the phone for a moment, then opened it again. Dialed. One ring. Two. "Hello?"

"Hey, Janie? It's Beth."

"Oh, hi! I was just starting to wonder where you are."

"I had a couple of errands to run after work. Figured I'd better let you know I'll be a little longer. Don't wait to eat if you're hungry."

"I'm good for now. I think I'll take both dogs to the park for a romp if that's okay with you."

"That's great, Clover would love it."

"Is her ball in the usual place?"

"Should be. I really appreciate this."

"No problem. I'll see you when you get home."

I pocketed the phone and got out of the car, stretching casually as though I'd been sitting too long. From behind the veil of my wig I surveyed the surrounding houses. In the waning light of late afternoon, a couple of living room windows glowed with the blue light of television. I could see no movement, no twitch of a curtain with a watcher behind. I locked the car and strolled down the street to the house I'd been watching.

It was dark and still, but no need to take unnecessary chances. I rang the doorbell, which made an unpleasant grating buzz from within. After a minute I rang again, then knocked. No answer.

I took another quick survey of the surrounding houses, then left the porch, passed the double garage door, and followed an informal path of paving stones around to the right. There were no windows along that side of the garage, just the plain stucco wall.

I emerged around the corner into the backyard and gave a little smile. A deck stretched the full width of the house. The central square of grass below it hadn't been mown recently. The landscaping consisted mainly of easy-care shrubs and evergreens designed to give maximum privacy from the eyes of the neighbors.

I felt a bit safer.

A plain door gave access to the garage; I tried the knob. Locked. Beyond that, sliders that led onto the deck were covered with vertical blinds, but one of the slats was askew. I peered inside. The wedge I could see appeared to be a combination dining and family room, with a brick fireplace on the back wall. I could see the end of a kitchen counter to the right.

The place was empty. No furniture at all, though a thick porcelain coffee mug sat on the fireplace mantel.

I tried the sliding door, but as expected it was locked. I looked more closely to see if I could discern anything that looked like a security system, but I had no idea what I should look for. It seemed to be an ordinary slider.

I moved to the next window; it had a cotton valance printed with a cheerful design of tea pots and cups, but no curtain. The kitchen sink was below the window. Further along was small window with frosted glass, probably a bathroom, then another slider. I figured this must lead into the master bedroom.

I stepped off the deck to peer around the last side of the house. Two more sash windows, both too high up to see into. I turned to the back yard to look for something useful.

A little shed in the back corner was unlocked but completely empty. It had been prettied up with a surrounding flower bed at some time in the past. Now the bed held only an assortment of happy weeds. But someone had created a border with bricks set at an angle into the dirt. I grabbed one and tugged. It didn't budge.

I looked further and saw that a couple of bricks were out of alignment. Possibly they'd been dislodged by a power mower or other yard equipment. I gave one a tentative nudge with my foot; it moved. I grasped this one and pulled and it flew up as though it had wings. I nearly fell over backwards but managed just to stumble and reel for a moment, glad for the privacy the surrounding greenery gave. I felt a sardonic smile twist my lips.

You can catch me breaking and entering, but please do not observe me falling on my ass.

15

I carried the brick to the slider into the master bedroom. The surrounding shrubbery seemed a bit thicker here. I grasped one end of the brick and brought the other down onto the glass by the door handle.

The brick chipped. The door did not.

I gripped the brick harder and tried again. To my nervous ears the sound was horrifically loud, but the glass didn't break. And no one shouted at me or came running.

Raw frustration burned in my throat. I thought of that woman sitting in the office that should be mine, using my money, pretending to be me. I wrapped my shirt tail around the brick for a better grip. I thought of my car exploding in a field of tiny trees. I thought of my sister.

Half turning, I brought the brick down in a backward arc.

Door glass shattered, bouncing against the vertical blinds and showering the carpet below. I reached inside carefully and flicked up the door lock, praying as I did so that whoever owned the house had not put a three-foot wooden dowel in the slider track to prevent it being opened. I tugged on the door handle. Silently it slid open.

I pushed the blinds apart and stepped in, avoiding the broken glass.

This room was as empty as the family room. Beige walls, beige carpets. Mirrored closet doors. An open door to the left showed a beige bathroom with a glass-enclosed shower.

The air smelled stale. No one had been here in some time, and certainly no fresh air had been allowed to enter. The silence lay as stagnant as the air. I tiptoed to the open door to the hallway.

The sightline ran straight to the kitchen and dining area. It was nearly dark outside, and the house was even darker. I took a deep breath and flipped a light switch in the hall. A single ceiling fixture in the middle came on. The bulb's wattage was too low to shine very brightly though the opaque glass of the fixture, but it was plenty of light to navigate by. I hoped it couldn't be seen from outside.

Three doors on the right, one on the left. All closed. From its position I deduced the left hand door was the bathroom with the frosted glass window. I was betting that the closed door across from it was a linen closet.

I pushed open the first door I came to and peeked in; an empty bedroom. Down the hall—linen closet, indeed, behind door number two, with bathroom opposite. I approached the last door, and though I was sure no one was there, it was still very hard to make myself open that door. I breathed in some of the stale air, turned the knob, and pushed slowly. Light from the hall crept in and showed piles of irregular shapes. I looked across the room to make sure that the short draperies over the single window on the front wall were closed. I flipped on the light.

The irregular shapes were boxes and furniture.

Boxes and furniture I had last seen on a moving van parked outside my house in North Carolina.

The furniture was piled into a corner of the room, pieces stacked on top of one another randomly. The upholstered chair and ottoman had both been slashed and stuffing pulled out. The mattress had suffered the same fate. Desk drawers had been pulled out dumped onto the floor.

The rest of the space was occupied by cartons, all with their carefully taped tops slashed open. Every box had been roughly searched. The contents had been piled back into some, but others disgorged clothing, kitchen equipment, and books onto the floor. One of the bath towels embroidered with ducklings that my sister had given me two Christmases ago lay across the carpet, the outline of a booted foot impressed in it.

I held onto the door knob, waiting for a surge of dizziness to pass. When my head felt steadier, I stepped carefully into the room, moving among the boxes, peeking into one or two.

I remembered my last weeks in North Carolina, deciding what I would bring to Oregon, what I would store. I knew I'd be working long hours and that my apartment would be small. I deliberately chose the most practical things to bring west. The antiques, the mementos, the family photo albums were all still behind locked doors of a storage facility a few miles from my old home. But I'd brought favorite books that now lay with pages crumpled, shorn of their dust jackets; china dishes I'd found in Raleigh in a second-hand store that had been full of sunbeams and dust motes; the cast iron skillet in which our dad had fried potatoes for Sunday breakfasts that came out crisp and brown on one side. I had brought along what I hoped would be just the right number of memories.

I couldn't bring myself to touch anything. The memories would have to be enough. My eyes stung with tears as I looked at the chaos.

I left the house, turning off the bedroom light, then the hall light as I passed the switches, closing the sliding door and relocking it even though anyone could reach in as I had done to open it. Full darkness had come, bringing the nighttime chill I was not yet accustomed to. A short shadow cast by a street light accompanied me to the car. I drove slowly to the parking space behind Janie's store, then let myself into the building with the key she'd given me.

Clover's glad barking erupted and she met me on the stairs, wagging so hard her back feet danced. A shadow fell on us and I looked up to see Janie and Tuffy silhouetted against the hall light.

"Hi! How was your day?" she asked cheerfully.

"Oh, just a day." I finished climbing the stairs and gave her a smile.

"Wait till you taste dinner. If you had 'just a day' then dinner will definitely be the high point."

Saturday afternoon was the perfect fall day, sunny and crisp with a hint of a breeze. Business at the thrift store ground to a halt by two-thirty, and by three-thirty Janie grabbed the "Closed" sign and hung it up in the window.

"Can you do that?" I asked, a little shocked.

"Heck yeah. What's the point of owning the store if you can't close it when you feel like it? Come on, let's grab the dogs and take them to the park."

The dog park was lively with happy dogs and their owners. Janie knew many of them and gave me a verbal tour when no one could hear us. She pointed with her chin to a young man throwing balls for his blue heeler. "He's an FBI agent, and his dog is deaf."

"Wow."

"And the woman with the Chesapeake Bay retriever over there is an artist. She did the most amazing picture book with cut paper illustrations. I've given it to every preschooler I know."

"Lucky preschoolers." I gave Clover's ball a high underhanded throw; she leapt straight up and caught it five feet above the ground.

We strolled down the field, throwing balls for Clover and watching Tuffy sucking scents into his eager nose. Janie pointed out the head of the local Democratic Party, a Salem police officer, two real estate agents, a high school music teacher, and the woman who cut her hair. Mentally I paired them with their counterparts in my hometown, smiling inwardly at the contrasts and the matches.

"Oh, look, there's my vet." She waved to a slender woman with curly hair who was throwing balls for a beautiful German shepherd.

A man's voice shouted behind us. "Mary Claire! Janie!"

We turned to see Andy hurrying toward us with a tiny, fluffy brown dog running circles around him.

"Andy! Piper!" Janie waved enthusiastically. I threw another ball for Clover and watched Andy with a smile. "I haven't seen you for ages," she added when he was close enough for normal speech.

"We went by the thrift store to see if you guys wanted to come with us to the dog park but the place was closed."

"Slow day."

"I've always thought that instead of getting to stay home in bad weather, we should get a certain number of clement weather days a year," I told them.

"Great idea. Perfect for a place like Salem that doesn't get a ton of snow. I'll suggest it to Valerie Monday when I get to work."

"This is your dog?" I asked.

"Yes, meet Piper. I know, he's ridiculous. Piper! Stop that!"

The little guy had run up behind a black lab and was trying his best to be tall enough to hump the creature. The lab gave him a look of disdain over her shoulder and walked away.

"He's so embarrassing." Andy shook his head. "Talk about delusions of grandeur."

Clover returned with the ball and dropped it on my foot. I picked it up with the Chuckit with the ease of long practice.

"Your dog?" Andy asked.

I opened my mouth to say yes, but Janie barreled in ahead of me.

"No, this is Clover. She belongs to another friend of mine. She had to leave her with me for a few weeks and Mary Claire has been great, helping keep her exercised."

I threw the ball, keeping my face turned away from Andy to give my pink cheeks a chance to cool. I couldn't believe the mistake I'd nearly made. Clover ran out, anticipating the landing point of the ball and catching it on the first bounce.

"Nice dog," he said. "I bet she has a lot of energy."

"That she does," Janie said. "So how have you been?"

"Pretty good. I've got this great new assistant at work. Hey, I guess I have you to thank for her, right?"

"Yup, well, me and Valerie. But I didn't know you were working there until Mary Claire came home her first day and told me."

"Yeah, I guess I started at WETCo not long after the last play we did together."

A woman with a large black dog came into view at the far end of the track that went around the back part of the dog park. Lisa and Chester. I nudged Janie and gave a little nod in their direction, hoping we could immediately start for the parking lot. Lisa had seen me in this very place playing with my dog just a few days ago. Any confidence I had in my disguise immediately disappeared.

Janie broke off in mid-sentence. For a moment she looked as appalled as I felt. She started to turn so we could escape, but it was already too late.

"Janie!" Chester trotted up, Lisa close behind. Clover came running to greet them, ball still in her mouth. "How are you? I see you still have Clover with you."

"Hi, Lisa. Yes, she's still here. She and Tuffy get along great. How have you all been?"

"Don't get me started. If you hear I've killed my husband I hope you'll tell everyone he deserved it." She was laughing as she shook her head.

"I know what you mean. Lisa, do you know Andy?"

Lisa shook her head. "I think I've seen you out here with your dog though. Little floofy thing, right?"

"Yes, the little floofy thing that tries to hump all the girl dogs. It's so embarrassing." Andy sketched a little wave at her. "In fact, here he comes."

Piper ran up behind Clover and attempted his usual routine. She didn't even notice he was there, and he returned to the ground with a crestfallen expression. Clover turned to me and dropped her ball on my foot.

I tried to think how people who don't live around dogs would talk to them. "Good doggie," I said as insincerely as I could. Slowly I bent down and picked up the ball, which was covered with dog spit and dirt. I stuck out my tongue in disgust and laboriously pushed it into the flinger. Stepping away from the others, I gave it a halfhearted throw, which as I expected did not eject the ball. I tried again.

"Throw really hard, Mary Claire," Janie coached. I tried again and managed to lob the ball about four feet.

Clover brought the ball back and dropped it on Janie's foot. I handed her the Chuckit and saw that Andy was giving me a look that included one raised eyebrow. Janie picked up the ball with the tool and threw it an impressive distance.

"And have you met Mary Claire? Bill's cousin from Seattle."

"I don't think so. Welcome to Salem, Mary Claire."

"Hi. Errr, thanks." I peeked at her through the wig's wispy bangs and managed a shy smile, then let my gaze drop to the ground. In my peripheral vision I caught Andy shifting his weight from foot to foot, then kneeling to pet his tiny dog.

Lisa turned back to Janie. "Say, have you heard from Beth?"

Janie shook her head. "I had a lovely thank you card in the mail the other day, but nothing since then. You?"

"So you haven't heard what happened?"

I kept the same stupid smile on my face, but my brain was reeling. What could have happened to Beth that I didn't know about? A little stab of hope pierced me; maybe something had happened to the Fake Beth.

"No, did something happen to her?" Janie sounded mildly curious and concerned, the perfect note for someone she'd only known a short time.

"Darren found the news item online this morning. Remember she said she'd put most of her stuff in storage before she came to Oregon?"

I tried to remember if I'd told her and Darren that. Probably. Hard to keep all the stories straight.

"Yeah, I think she said that. Why?"

"Evidently the storage place was bombed. Can you believe that?"

"What?"

Lisa nodded enthusiastically. "Actually bombed. They thought it was centered on the unit with her stuff, but it took out half the row so they're not sure. The article said they hadn't been able to get hold of her for a comment, but one of her neighbors was quoted as saying she had emptied her house before she left so she could rent it. I guess she had all kinds of antiques and..."

Her voice faded away. My peripheral vision went black and I swayed on my feet. I concentrated on simply standing. That was all I had to do at this moment. Just stay on my feet in the middle of a grassy field in Salem, Oregon, with sunshine on my back and a small brown dog a few feet away trying to hump a basset hound. Just stay on my feet. And remember to breathe once in a while. I could do that. Maybe.

Lisa's voice faded back in. "...tried to call her, but she's never answered."

The shock in Janie's voice was genuine. "My god, that poor girl. Did it happen after she flew back?"

"I think so."

"I'm sure she'll be in touch soon. I wish she could have taken Clover with her. I'm sure she needs that comfort."

"At least you're keeping Clover safe. As soon as you hear from her be sure to let her know we're thinking about her."

"I will. Thanks for letting me know about it."

"I hate to break such bad news, but I figured you needed to know. I tell you, I've seen people having rough times, but I have never heard of anything like Beth Harding's bad luck."

Andy's eyes flew to Lisa's face. "Beth—"

"We'd better get going." Janie raised her voice to cover Andy's. I saw her step on his foot. "Tell Darren I said hello."

143

"Will do. I think Chester and I better make one more trip around the track." She looked around for her dog, who was several feet away, accepting treats from a young couple with a baby in a back pack.

"Mary Claire? Are you ready to go? Where's Tuffy?" She raised her voice as she got us moving. "Tuffy! Here, boy! Come on, you dog you."

Tuffy and Clover followed us up the field, and Andy scooped up Piper and held him close as he brought up the rear. I concentrated on walking, the no-longer-simple act of putting one foot in front of the other. A dirt clod nearly brought me down, but Andy and Janie both grabbed me. Neither of them said anything until we reached Janie's car. I opened the back door to let the dogs in, then turned to the others.

"What time does the sun set today?"

Janie clearly thought I'd lost my mind. Andy just seemed puzzled. "Ummm, about seven fifteen, seven thirty. Why?"

I shook my head. Not enough time. "Have either of you seen a weather report for tomorrow?"

"Supposed to be like today," Janie said. "Sunny. Nice. Are you okay?"

I met her eyes. "Not awfully, but don't worry. I will be."

She put her hand on my wrist and gave it a squeeze. Andy watched in silence.

"I—I need to tell you both something. Show you. Do you know someplace we could go and be away from town, somewhere out in the country where no one would be around?"

144

"Sure," Andy nodded. "Some friends of my parents have a ranch between here and the coast."

"And absolutely no one else would be there?"

"Very unlikely. We could take one of the farm tracks to a back pasture. There might be some goats. Would goats be okay?"

I nodded. "Goats will be fine. Just no people. How long a drive?"

"Mmm, forty minutes, another twenty or so once we leave the road."

"It's too late to do it today. Can you both go tomorrow?" Nods. "Good. Andy, meet us at Janie's store at nine."

16

I assumed that sleep would be a long time coming that night; that I would lie staring at the ceiling counting my losses like prayer beads on a string of memory. I retired to my room before nine, fleeing both the sympathy in Janie's eyes and the comfort foods she was intent on feeding me.

Clover knew something had happened. She dogged my footsteps even more closely than usual. When I sat at Janie's table eating dinner, she settled on my foot. And when I sank onto the couch she was draped across my lap almost before I had a lap. I pleaded exhaustion and took Clover across the hall to our refuge in Jasper's room.

We climbed the spiral stairs and settled into bed. Clover curled up and tucked her chin into her flank so that she resembled a smooth, round, dog-shaped river stone. She heaved a loud sigh that was close to a groan and closed her eyes.

"You said it," I told her, rubbing one of her soft, warm ears. I breathed out my own sigh and closed my eyes, ready to sink into a pool of grief.

A memory of my sister swam up from the depths of my brain. Kindergarten. The second or third day of school. I had taken my favorite book with me, a talisman in the same way that other young children might carry a favorite blanket or doll. During the free-for-all before the morning bell rang, Susie Higgins the mayor's little daughter walked up to me and grabbed my book out of my hands. She walked away with an indecently triumphant expression and started banging desks, chairs and other children with the book.

She only got to bang things for about a minute. My sister ran up behind her, grabbed the collar of her dress and yanked, then extracted the book from her hands.

"This is my *sister's* book," she had growled.

We had no more trouble with Susie.

I thought perhaps a book would be a good distraction now. The one I'd been reading earlier was lying by my pillow, but to my surprise my eyelids soon drooped and began to glue themselves closed for the night. I lay the book in the little niche in the wall and turned off the reading light. Curled around my dog, her comforting warmth permeated my core. We slept.

I was driving through Boston in a car whose windshield kept getting smaller and smaller. I grew more and more frightened as my vision was obscured, but I couldn't stop the car. On the radio, the Kingston Trio was singing, "Will he ever return? No, he never returned, and his fate is still unknown..." My sister sat in the passenger seat, talking happily about flying to Jamaica. She wore jeans and a sweater that had been her absolute favorite when we were at college. She seemed completely unaware of the way the windshield was disappearing, and in that horrible way that happens in dreams I couldn't force a single word from my throat.

That was all I could remember when I woke up.

But when I rubbed the dregs of sleep from my eyes and registered the pale early-morning light creeping into the high-ceilinged room, I knew where I had seen the Fake Beth before.

I sat in the back seat of Janie's car for the ride into the country. Andy had tried to get me to take the front, but I said I needed to think. All three dogs were back there with me. Andy had called the family friends who owned the ranch to make sure it was okay for us to be there. He told them I had just moved to town and he and Janie wanted to take me for a picnic. He'd even remembered to ask if the dogs would be a problem. Reportedly they were quite happy to let us enjoy the back reaches of their ranch, and gave Andy directions that would take us down a farm track along a picturesque creek to a hill with a panoramic view of the Coast Range.

As soon as she heard the word "picnic" Janie cried, "Good idea!" and began to pack a basket of food, now stowed in the trunk. With it was the small backpack I had borrowed to bring the equipment I would need, plus a large stainless steel bowl and a gallon jug of water for the dogs. Janie made one more trip inside and added a large plaid wool blanket to our equipment.

"It's not a picnic without a picnic blanket," she explained.

I nodded and gave her a smile. I was about to sever all ties with my old life. Might as well make a picnic of it.

We crossed the Willamette on the bridge that led from downtown Salem to the west side of town, then turned right and drove north along the river. In a very short time we had left town behind and were driving past farms that grew everything from hazelnuts to wine grapes to corn to nursery trees.

One bright green field exuded a familiar scent, but I couldn't think what it was. Before I could ask, Janie sniffed appreciatively and said, "Mmmm, spearmint. They must be harvesting." All three dogs had their noses up, testing the air on hyper-drive.

In a few miles Andy directed Janie to turn left onto a paved but narrow two-lane road. I settled back and watched the scenery, farms and fields and mailboxes. I noticed the names Henderson, Blalock, Scheidemann, Garcia.

Janie and Andy conversed in the front seat, but it was hard to keep track of what they were saying from the back. I caught the occasional word— pony...theater...WETCo...tomorrow—but the words flowed over and past me like the scent from the newly mown hay fields we passed. Saying I wanted to ride in back to think was a half-truth; mostly I did not want to talk. I rode numbly, hoping that I was not going to put them into terrible danger. Hoping they were the people I thought they were.

My head felt hot, suffocated. I reached up to scratch surreptitiously under the edge of the wig.

The road entered a belt of trees and dipped down to cross a single lane bridge. Andy pointed to the left, and Janie slowed the car to turn onto a dirt track. There had been no rain for weeks, so the surface was firm and fairly smooth. A cloud of dust rose behind us. The track led through a tunnel of trees taking advantage of the water source. I noticed a willow leaning over the water, leaves swirling in the slow autumn current. A maple leaf floated down, twisting through a shaft of sunlight.

I scanned the scenery as we passed, looking for any signs that other people were about. We followed the creek for about half a mile, then the track led away from the water, up a hill and down again, and through a farm gate. Andy jumped out to swing it open, then carefully closed it behind the car.

"Not much farther," he announced as he climbed back into his seat. "I think we skirt the edge of this field and then the track goes up to the top of the next hill."

The pastures around us were clothed with some kind of naturally low-growing grass that was a rich gold color. The hills appeared to be covered with velvet. I caught movement in my peripheral vision and tensed, but then I saw a herd of about fifteen goats grazing in the sun. They lifted their heads to watch us pass, still chewing.

In a few minutes we started up hill, and at the crest Andy announced, "This looks good." He turned in his seat. "Will this be okay for what you need?"

"It's perfect," I assured him. Janie stopped the car and we clicked off our seat belts. I opened my door and the dogs flowed over me, eager to get to all the exciting smells they could taste on the air. I followed more slowly, stretching as I looked around.

The view was stunning. Cultivated fields alternated with pasture land, fading off to the west into the undulations of the coastal mountains. The hill on which we stood dipped down to a grove of gigantic oak trees.

"Shall we picnic in the shade?" Janie asked, pointing to the oaks.

"Sure." I looked around and decided which direction I wanted to walk. "I need to set up some equipment over there. It won't take very long. Want help with the basket first?"

"Who needs my help?" Andy volunteered.

"I need to do this myself, but after I set up there will be some waiting time. Maybe while we're waiting we can see what feast Janie whipped up this morning. While we eat I'll start bringing both of you up to speed."

I left them toting the blanket and basket and dog supplies down to the shade. Slinging the little pack over my shoulder, I whistled for my dog and headed in the opposite direction. All three dogs came running, Piper straining to keep up with the bigger guys. We climbed the rise to the very top of the hill. I turned to make sure that I was in view of the picnic spot, then did a slow full circle, searching again for any signs of other people. I saw the patch of goats, still grazing in roughly the same location. Far off in the direction we had come from I saw a large barn with a silo, and near it a metal-roofed equipment shed. A red tailed hawk floated high above on a convenient thermal. Nothing else moved.

I settled cross-legged on the ground and opened the back pack. I had decided to assemble the device on site rather than bring it already put together. One by one I freed each piece from its bubble wrap, their smooth, intricate shapes as familiar as my own fingerprints. The wrappings went back into the pack to be reused later. I slotted each component into place, feeling as much as hearing the small click as they were joined. As many times as I had done this, I still felt a little glow of pride at the elegance of the design.

When I had assembled all the parts that had been in the pack, I called Clover. She left whatever enticing smell she and Tuffy and Piper were enjoying and came running, tail on high. "Hey, baby girl, I need to borrow your collar for a minute."

I clicked open the clasp and took the collar off her neck. She gave herself a thorough shake, ears flapping loudly. Running a fingertip along the edge, I located the slightly thicker section I was looking for. With my nail I pried open the Velcro hidden there, and three tiny silver disks fell into my hand. These I tucked into their cavity in the assembled device and closed the hatch securely. I looped Clover's collar back around her neck and closed the clasp.

"Thanks, sweetie," I told her and patted her shoulder. She went running back to her friends.

I turned the device around in my hands. It wasn't large, a black plastic box with rounded corners, six inches by eight by eight. It was smooth on all sides; anyone who didn't know where the openings were would spend a long time looking. I flicked open a tiny covering on one of the short sides, pressed the button hidden there, and closed it up again. Then I carefully placed the device on the ground.

So small a thing to be so wonderful, and so dangerous.

Rising, I called to the dogs and headed back down the hill to where the plaid blanket was spread upon the ground.

"All set?" Janie asked me when I reached them. I nodded.

"All set. It takes a little while to activate. All this fresh air is making me hungry. What's for lunch?"

We settled on the blanket and Janie handed out plates of food. I leaned my back against the trunk of the tree and nibbled on a piece of cheese. It had no flavor, but since I had claimed to be hungry I needed to eat something.

I was well placed to keep an eye on my device; the others had their backs to the hill.

"I hardly know where to start," I confessed. "But I guess it should be with this: what I'm going to tell you could be dangerous. For you. As in life-and-death dangerous. Janie, you have a son to consider. Andy, you have family and friends who love you."

"Not to mention my rewarding work at WETCo." He gave me a cheeky grin.

"I think I can trust you both. I really hope so, and heaven help me if I'm wrong. But I don't have anything more to lose. It's down to my dog and my life."

Janie's eyes were great pools of sympathy. "And I, for one, will help you defend both of those."

Andy nodded. "I'm in."

"Thanks." I paused to swallow. "Okay. Maybe the next thing is this." I reached up and pulled off the wig and flung it to the corner of the blanket, then gave my head a good rub. "Man, that feels good. So yes, Andy, I have been in disguise."

"I was pretty sure it was a wig, but hey, none of my business. Maybe you've had cancer or something."

"I guess things really can always get worse. No, not cancer. But the wig wasn't the only part of the disguise. My name isn't really Mary Claire Johnson. It's Beth Harding."

He sat up straighter and put down his plate. "You mean—"

I nodded. "You were quite right about that woman at Willamette Environmental having a fake Southern accent. In fact, if y'all don't mind I'd like to reclaim my own voice for now." I dropped back into the accent I'd

154

grown up with. "She's been impersonating me. More than impersonating. She's stolen my life."

I quickly sketched in the events from my time on Mount Hood to discovering the hijacking of all my passwords, to the cancellation of my apartment and the theft of my moving van. I described the ATM from hell that ate my debit card and the inability of the bank manager to help.

"The woman we met at the dog park yesterday, Andy? Lisa?" He nodded. "Her husband was waiting to use the ATM and when I kicked it in a fit of temper he told me not to break the thing. I said it had eaten my card and I didn't have much cash left and could he recommend a cheap motel, and he ended up inviting me to stay in their little guest cottage. I was there a couple of nights—"

"And then Beth and I met at the dog park," Janie added. "When I heard she was homeless and nearly penniless, and Jasper had just gone off to college and there was his empty room, well, I forced her to come stay with me."

I gave her a grateful smile. "I seem to recall the deal was I would earn my room and board by helping at the thrift store. And then the first thing I did was almost get you killed."

Andy gaped. "Killed?"

"My first night at Janie's we took the dogs to the park. When we left we decided to take a drive down River Road. Someone had tampered with the brakes on my car and they failed."

"She was amazingly cool," Janie added. "Totally did not panic. We ended up going in circles in a field of baby Christmas trees. Then the car exploded—"

"After we got out."

"—and burned up. That's when she told me about the woman who stole her life and was impersonating her at Willamette Environmental. And I remembered that Valerie worked there in HR so I called her and told her the sad story about Mary Claire losing her purse and all her ID cards and how badly she needed a job—"

"And Valerie is after all the one with nine cats and a three-legged iguana," Andy finished for her. "So Mary Claire enters my life and very soon is showing interest in the other new employee, the annoying woman in the office on the secure floor with the Southern accent she keeps forgetting to use. The one bringing some big project to the company that the head honchos expect to bring in major money. A project that office scuttlebutt says is not progressing in any way."

"Well, duh," said Janie with masterly sarcasm. "How could it when she's not the real Beth Harding?"

"No one will ever make any progress on the project without me." I shifted my position on the blanket, leaning forward. "It's true that they have my working files because I sent them ahead, and yes, I know how incredibly stupid that was. But...I didn't send them everything."

"That's the smartest thing you've done in this whole mess," Janie told me frankly.

"But Mary Claire—I mean Beth—er, I don't know what to call you now. I mean, I'm sure you really are Beth, but for the past couple of weeks I thought of that other person as Beth, and—"

"Mary Claire is fine. I've gotten to rather like Mary Claire."

"Okay, Mary Claire it is."

"And your question was...?"

"My question was, what's this project you were bringing to WETCo?"

"Yes," said Janie, "I am dying of curiosity. Please, please tell us."

I looked beyond them to the hillside where I had set up my device. As I had hoped, the timing was perfect. I gestured for them to look behind them.

"I can make it rain."

17

Janie leapt to her feet, then stood where she was, unable to move. Andy gaped. I pushed myself up using the trunk of the tree I'd been leaning on and walked to Janie's side, taking in the sight.

At the top of the golden hill where I had placed the device, a column of rain about twenty feet in diameter fell from the sky. All around it the sun still shone, but the circle of rain fell steadily straight down from a cloud that had formed above it. We could see through the rain as though it were a scrim curtain for a dream sequence in a stage play. Because of the angle of our line of sight, a rainbow curved over the vision.

"I'd better go turn it off," I said after a couple of minutes. "It would be best if no one else sees it."

I walked up the hill, the dogs gamboling about my feet. At the edge of the rain I paused, thinking I should have brought an umbrella, before remembering my umbrella had been on the floor behind the driver's seat of my car. Oh well, it was a warm day, I would dry soon.

I stepped into the rain. It was just rain, regular rain, cool on my skin, like any rain would be this time of year. The short dry grasses beneath my feet were soaked and already seemed a bit revived by the water. I walked to the little box, picked it up, opened the hidden compartment and pressed the button. The smallest possible tremor from within the box ceased. In eight...nine...ten seconds the rain diminished, then stopped. I looked up and watched the last of the cloud fade into nothingness.

Movement caught my eye. Janie had followed me, and Andy was a few feet behind her. They walked into the circle of wet grass and did a slow turn. Janie leaned over and laid her hand flat on the wet ground. Tuffy ran up and applied his nose to some scent that had been enhanced by getting wet.

"What...how..." Janie shook her head as she stood up again. "I can't..."

"I know. Really, I know. Come on. I need to put this away. I left the backpack down by the tree."

I led them back to our picnic blanket and sat again by the oak. My fingers went to work taking the device apart; I hardly needed to look as I worked, having done this so many times. Like sleepwalkers the others sank down in the places they had occupied before. No one spoke. A bee buzzed by; from the other side of the hill floated a querulous "Maaa-aaa-aaa"

159

from a goat. I disassembled the box, carefully wrapping each piece in its bubble wrap shroud and stowing them in the pack. The three tiny silver disks I palmed and then slid into a pocket; I'd hide them again in Clover's collar when no one was looking.

Andy finally gave a loud sigh. "That was the most amazing thing I've ever seen. I mean—the implications are just staggering."

"I've been struggling with them for several years. Ever since my sister and I first started talking about the possibility."

"This is...this is a god-like power."

"Yes. And I'm no god. But even less so the people I'm up against."

"We're up against." Janie spoke at last. Her expression was grim. "You're not in this alone."

"I should be. I tried to be. But you're both in it now."

"Maybe we need more people, not less. Maybe you should go public," Andy suggested. I shifted uncomfortably.

"Mmmm, maybe, but—I don't think so. Not yet. For one thing, we'd be besieged. It's not that I don't want to share the technology, that's why I decided to work with Willamette Environmental to turn the small prototype into a usefully-sized device that could be available on the open market. But if news of even the prototype leaks out, every government, every company in every drought-ridden part of the planet will be trying to grab it."

"Chaos," Janie said. "Worse than chaos. There isn't a government or a black marketer on earth that wouldn't kill in a heartbeat for this."

"The only reason I'm still alive," I told them, "is because at this point no one else can duplicate my device. Yes, there are plans and schematics and working documents, but crucial parts are still only in my head. But if the prototype were to fall into the wrong hands, eventually someone would probably be able to reverse-engineer it. And then—and then they will kill me." My throat tightened, but I went on. "They will kill me...just as they killed my sister."

18

"She was struck down in her own home by an intruder." After one look at the shock on their faces, I had to lower my eyes. "Her house was ransacked and files were stolen. They took other stuff as well, probably to make it look like a regular burglary that went bad. She was in a coma for several days, and then she died."

I pushed away the image of that hospital room, and the terrible silence when the final machine was turned off.

"Oh, Beth," Janie said. "How awful. How long ago?"

"Almost five months. About the time I was interviewing with Willamette Environmental. I've spent every day since then expecting to be next. But they must have realized that they don't have everything they need yet. Maybe this whole crazy business of impersonating me was to buy time. Or discredit me. I mean, right now no one but you two would believe I'm really Beth Harding, and the imposter's ineptitude in working on the project is tarnishing that. It won't take long for the powers that be at Willamette Environmental to want to see some progress, and when there hasn't been any they're going to fire her. Whoever is doing this must not want the project to be developed by this company. Maybe they have their own company or they've been hired by someone to get hold of the project. Or maybe Willamette Environmental is behind it all and the CEO has some grand scheme to cut me out of the picture and have everything. Or..."

Another detail occurred to me. I stared into space, turning it around in my mind.

"Or what?" Andy prompted.

"I just thought about the patent. I own the patent, but if they succeed in replacing me, then the Fake Beth could even have that."

Janie sat up straighter. "Okay, that's it. Enough already."

"I beg your pardon?"

"I mean enough of these people and their shenanigans. *Enough*. They have lied and cheated and killed, all in the name of greed. They are trying to steal something that could be used for good, to help people, and heaven only knows what their plans are once they have it. I'm pretty sure it won't be for anything positive."

163

"Agreed," Andy added.

"So we are going after them and they are not going to know what hit them." She gave me a grim smile. "I told you we are going to nail that woman's ass, and I meant it."

"Amen to that," Andy said. "The time for dealing with this alone is past. With three of us we should be able to do some damage."

"I really, *really* want to do some damage to her. Them." Janie's voice was fierce with passion. "When— when Bill died, there was absolutely nothing I could do. He fought the disease, but he lost. Cancer won. I lost the love of my life, and I could do *nothing* to stop it."

I nodded at her. I knew about that kind of helplessness.

"Don't you see?" she went on. "Yes, I still have a son. But he is safely in Vermont. I need to help make them pay. *Someone* is going to pay."

Tears glittered on her eyelashes. I reached out to touch her knee.

"I think we've got a real chance," Andy went on after a moment. "Two of us have access to the Fake Beth every day at work. Do you think they suspect that Mary Claire is you in disguise?"

"I don't *think* so," I said slowly. "I'm hyper-aware of her at work, but she barely registers me. I'm just a mail clerk. But there's still something I haven't told you. Janie, you remember me saying I thought I'd seen her somewhere before?"

"Yes, sure, I thought maybe you'd noticed her peripherally, that she'd been following you."

I shook my head. "Maybe she was, but I finally pinned down the memory of seeing her before. Actually, I think it was a dream that did it."

"So who is she?"

"Her name is Carlie Wilkinson, and we went to the same college. She was a year behind us, I think."

"Us?" Andy looked puzzled.

"My sister Georgette and me."

"You started college the same time?"

"Well, sure. We're twins. I thought I said so."

They both shook their heads. "Identical twins?" Janie asked.

"Yes. Very, actually. Our mom could tell us apart, but dad always faked it. We let him think he always got it right."

"Losing a sibling is always hard, but a twin...I can't imagine."

I had to look down, blinking hard for a moment. "Yeah. Anyway, I don't think we ever had any classes with her, but I'm pretty sure that's who she is. Allowing for the changes twenty years makes in everyone, and different hair style and such. But everyone knew who she was when she got kicked out."

"What for?" Andy shifted his position on the blanket and reached for a grape. "And where did you go to college, anyway?"

"M.I.T. And she was kicked out for cheating."

We put our first idea into action the next morning. Andy and I did our usual morning duties—sorting and delivering mail, which was heavier than usual since it included Saturday's delivery; getting packages ready to go out in the afternoon; stocking machines in The Bistro—with the added duty for Andy of finding his way into the company's online internal calendar. We wanted to keep an eye on any meetings that might have something to do with my device. When all had been taken care of, I called Janie.

"Were you able to set it up?"

"Of course. What time do you want it? I told them I'd get back to them on that."

"At eleven if at all possible. Her calendar is clear then and she should be in her office."

"Okay, I'll call them. If for some reason that won't work I'll let you know."

In a few minutes she called me back.

"Beth? It's on."

"Great. Keep your fingers crossed that I find something useful." I ended the call and looked at Andy. "We're set for eleven."

"You won't have much time up there."

"If you can, engage her in conversation before she heads back. You know, how do you like Oregon, have you been to the beach yet, this must be really different from North Carolina—"

By now he was laughing at me. "Mary Claire, I actually do know how to carry on a conversation, even with someone I can't stand."

166

"Okay, sorry. I know you can talk the hind leg off a hyena if you want to."

"Wonderful. Now I'll be thinking of hyenas every time I see her. Though come to think of it, what could be more appropriate?"

At about ten minutes before eleven, I made my way to the fifth floor, pushing one of the mail carts before me. We had loaded it with a couple of empty boxes that we had sealed and addressed so in case anyone noticed me wandering around I could appear to be making a delivery. I rolled the cart off the elevator and pushed it to the locked door that secured the floor, keyed in the code on the pad set into the wall, and continued through. Around the corner to the left, I moved the cart into a handy niche and left it there. Then I made my way to the ladies' room. I checked under the stall doors and was glad to see no one was there. I returned to the entry door and opened it a crack, peering out into the quiet hallway.

Fake Beth (I found I was still calling her that in my head rather than Carlie) would have to pass here on her way to the elevator, unless she took a convoluted route in the other direction. Once she was on the elevator I'd be on my way. I glanced at my watch; just about time for Andy to be calling her. My heart was beating faster than normal, and I deliberately slowed my breathing. Air in, air out, in through the nose, out through the mouth...After seemingly eons of time had passed I glanced at my watch again. Two minutes later than the last time I looked. I breathed out through my nose in disgust.

And then there she was, mincing along in a tight pencil skirt and very high heels. Good, she was not carrying her purse. But instead of walking straight to the elevator, she angled toward the ladies' room door. I flung myself away and into the furthest stall, clicking the latch just as I heard the door make its quiet closing thud behind her. I peeked through the narrow gap between my door and the frame and saw her pause in front of the mirror over the sinks. She leaned close to her reflection, damped a finger with spit and smoothed an eyebrow, checked her teeth for lipstick. She turned away from her image and moved toward the stalls and out of my sight, but from the subsequent sounds I knew where she was. The toilet flushed and she reappeared in my line of sight.

She turned on the hot water tap and lathered up her hands, and began to scrub. And scrub. And scrub. Good lord, the woman was headed for the mail room. Did she think she was going to be performing surgery down there? Finally she rinsed her hands—and then pumped on more soap and began to scrub again.

Lady Macbeth came to mind.

I was almost to the point of bursting out of my stall and screaming, "Stop washing already, you will never be able to scrub away your guilt!" But just then she rinsed once more, grabbed eleven paper towels from the dispenser, and began to dry each finger and nail individually.

It is fortunate that I do not carry a gun. I was willing by now to shoot her for the hand-washing routine alone, let alone everything else she had done.

The door to the hall opened, and Valerie Frost, the Human Resources lady, bustled in. She gave the Fake Beth a beaming smile.

"Well, good morning, Dr. Harding! How are you doing today?"

"I'm just fine, thanks." Fake Beth's smile was as false as her accent.

"Hasn't the weather been fabulous? Oh, that's right. You haven't lived through one of our Oregon winters yet, have you? I hope all the rain doesn't get to you."

"I'm sure I'll be fine."

"So how are you settling in? Are you liking Salem?"

"Oh yes, it's such a lovely town. Thanks."

Fake Beth tried to edge past Valerie. Valerie shifted her weight and somehow blocked Fake Beth from the door.

"Have you had a chance yet to see anything of our beautiful state? Been to the beach? No? Well, if you go straight west on highway twenty-two, you'll end up in Lincoln City. You can head north or south at that point and it's all just beautiful. I know North Carolina has its own beaches, but our coast is so rocky, I'm sure you'll be amazed at the difference.

"Thanks, I'll—"

"If you go north, you would probably enjoy Cannon Beach. Nice shops, some very good restaurants. And be sure to do the tour at the cheese factory in Tillamook. Or if you go south..." She paused to think.

"Oh, Beverly Beach State Park is lovely. Good parking, easy walk out onto the beach."

"I'll try it one of these days. Excuse me, I—"

"And how is your work going?"

The simple question stopped Fake Beth in her tracks. The temperature in the room seemed to drop ten degrees. I squinted through my little gap, and now Valerie's smile seemed precisely as false as the other woman's. Two heartbeats passed.

"It's going just great," Fake Beth said flatly. "Thank you so much for asking. Will you excuse me? I'm on my way down to the mail room. They called and said there's a delivery I have to sign for."

Valerie stepped aside. "Of course, Dr. Harding. You have a good day. And tell Andy down in the mail room I said hi."

When Fake Beth had gone, Valerie crossed her arms and stood staring at the closed door. Then she glanced at herself in the mirror, gave a little smile, and left.

As soon as the coast was clear, I left the bathroom and hurried down the hall. The door with the "Beth Harding" nameplate was locked, but Andy had given me a master key. "After all, the mail has to be delivered whether people are in their offices or not."

I looked around to make sure I was unobserved, and let myself through the door. Closing it softly behind me, I went first to the desk. The drawers had locks, but she had left the key sticking out of the top left hand one. I opened that drawer first. Office

170

supplies, stationery, a complete kit for re-doing her nails. The left lower drawer held two heavy-bottomed crystal glasses and a bottle of Macallan forty-year-old single malt Scotch. My eyebrows shot up. It was a pricey tipple to keep in a desk drawer at work.

The right-hand lower drawer held her purse, a roomy black crocodile bag with the Chanel emblem hanging from the handle. I grabbed it, glad she wasn't one of those women who carried a purse with them everywhere. I rifled through; make-up, more nail equipment, a packet of floss threaders, a roll of mints, two empty Ooshy Gooshy bar wrappers, a can of pepper spray, a cylindrical black leather case holding a pair of Etnia Barcelona sunglasses, three cheap stick pens, a tiny bottle of hand sanitizer, a hairbrush, a spritzer of Hermes perfume, and a hot pink Fendi wallet. I pulled the wallet out and set the purse on the desk.

Cash. Three hundred plus in twenties and assorted smaller bills. No change. Credit cards—all in the name of Beth Harding—for Nordstrom, Macy's, and Anthropologie as well as a couple of bank issued MasterCards, and a debit card for the checking account that was receiving her pay. Expiration dates were far enough into the future that these cards all had to be new. I flipped through the clear plastic windows until I came to a driver's license. As expected it was from North Carolina, with my name and her picture. This I slid out and pocketed. I dropped the wallet back into the purse and returned it to the drawer. The key went back into the lock where I had found it.

I rose from the desk chair and considered the file drawers in the built-in credenza under the window. Before I tried to open one, I decided to peek into the adjoining workroom. I cracked open the door and stuck my head in. The space was laid out exactly as I had requested, including the computer array and 3-D printer I had specified. A free-standing cupboard occupied the far corner. On the desktop near the printer were some oddly shaped pieces of black plastic. I walked over to have a closer look.

They had succeeded in extruding half a dozen pieces that corresponded to parts of my device at about a fifty percent increase in size. I picked one up and examined it.

Just then my phone vibrated in my pocket and I nearly dropped the component. It danced wildly in my fingers before I was able to carefully lay it down. I pulled out the phone.

"Yes?"

"Mary Claire, get out now! She left a few minutes ago, she'll be there soon."

"What! You were supposed to call me as soon as she started back to the elevator." I hurried to the workroom door as I talked.

"The office phone rang. I picked it up and tried to put them on hold, but it was the chairman of the board asking if a package he'd sent had arrived. By the time I got rid of him she'd gone."

"All right, I'm leaving."

I shut the phone and shoved it into my sweater pocket. Headed for the door to the hallway. Heard voices close by.

"Ah, Dr. Harding. Good morning. May I have a word?" A deep, resonant man's voice, one I had previously heard only over the telephone.

"Of course, Mr. Linder, please come in. Oh, would you mind holding these while I...? Thanks."

The sound of a key in the lock had me winging across the room, back into the workroom. I flicked off the light and scuttled to the cabinet in the corner.

"Please come in." Her accent fairly dripped with honey.

Martin Linder was the CEO of Willamette Environmental.

"Where would you like your lovely flowers? You must have an admirer."

I silently opened the cabinet door. The light from the double window opposite showed that it was empty except for a couple of black vinyl notebooks on an eye-level shelf.

"Just put them on the cabinet there. Perfect, thanks. They are pretty, aren't they? I'm afraid I'm not sure who sent them, the signature was rather illegible."

The lower half of the cabinet was empty. I thanked my unknowing foresight in specifying this piece of furniture; I'd been thinking I might have tall things to store. I'd never considered the possibility that I would be storing myself.

"Won't you sit down? Can I get you anything?"

"No, no, I'm fine, thanks. Just wanted to touch base and see how things are going."

I climbed into the cabinet and pulled the doors in, leaving them cracked a bit so that I could hear. And breathe. Thank heavens that claustrophobia was not one of my problems.

"It's early days, of course, but so far I think things are going well."

"You've found the office to your liking?"

"Oh yes. Very nice, and I really appreciate how quiet it is up here."

"There was no question but that we would locate you on our most secure floor."

Secure against everything except mail room personnel, I thought.

His mellifluous voice continued. "Is all your equipment up to your specs?"

"Oh yes. I couldn't be more pleased."

"And have you found any of your colleagues yet whom you would like to invite to be on your team?"

Yeah, I thought in my most sarcastic tone, how about that mail clerk? She knows a lot about this project.

"I'm afraid that's going a little slower." She injected a beseeching tone into her voice. I imagined her looking at him with puppy dog eyes. "As you know, it's of the utmost importance that I not only find colleagues who are trainable, but also understand the need for complete secrecy."

"I see. I was thinking we might set up a series of informal round table discussions, so that you can get a better idea of the caliber of our scientists and researchers. I'm sure I can vouch for any of them when it comes to security."

"That would be delightful, Mr. Linder. Very helpful. How clever of you to think of it."

"That's what we'll do then. I'll have my secretary consult you on the schedule. And if you don't mind, I may include an old friend in some of the discussions. He's the financial consultant I think I told you about."

"As long as he's aware of the importance of the project and assuring its security, then of course."

"Once the project is nearing the testing stage, we'll need to start pulling in venture capital for production. That's Darren's area of expertise."

I had a feeling I knew his friend Darren's last name. And that Fake Beth did as well.

"I'll look forward to meeting him. And I just want to say...thank you so much for your encouragement and support."

"Not at all." It sounded as though she had him on his feet and was moving him toward the door. "You've brought us an amazing project. I'll talk to you again soon."

I heard her office door close. Silence. Then she swept through the door into the workroom and strode to the table with the random components on it. Through the gap in the cabinet door I saw her rigid back and clenched fists. I felt like I had been looking at her through narrow gaps my whole life.

She raised both fists and brought them down on the components, scattering broken pieces in all directions. I flinched. But I didn't make a sound.

19

Janie and Andy and I met after work at a seedy-looking bar that Andy recommended. "A buddy of mine runs it," he'd said, "and he brews some great beers."

I didn't tell him I don't like beer, but when I saw the place I almost suggested we go somewhere else. I would certainly never have gone through those doors by myself. Janie pulled into the parking lot and climbed out of her car.

"You must be joking," she said to Andy, staring at the peeling paint and broken neon sign.

"Come on," he grinned, holding open the door, "just trust me. The place is in disguise. Just like Mary Claire."

So we walked through the splintering plywood hollow-core door into a small vestibule, then through the scrim of a clattering bead curtain and into a room that exuded a certain bohemian charm. There were three guys on stools at the bar sharing a bowl of popcorn and drinking beer from hefty mugs as they watched a soccer game on the TV mounted on the wall. Off to the right, two young women—one with hair so long that Rapunzel immediately came to mind—played what appeared to be an extremely serious game of pool. A few booths were occupied.

The bartender looked our way. "Hey, Betsy! How's it hanging?"

Andy waved at him and called, "Real good, Glen, real good."

"Betsy?" Janie looked at Andy questioningly.

He pointed to the back. "Looks like the last booth is empty. I'll grab some drinks."

"Ummm, I don't like beer," I confessed.

"Let me see what I can find for you."

We settled across from each other in the last booth, Janie with her back to the door. In a moment Andy showed up bearing a tray with three foaming glasses, which he proceeded to distribute.

"For moi, Glen's famous oatmeal stout, and for Janie, a cask ale regrettably named Hoppy Toffee. And Mary Claire gets a Willamette Wonder cider."

I tasted the bubbly, almost wine-colored liquid. "Wow. Good. What is it?"

"Hard cider. Glen brews it from local pears and blackberries. Be careful, it does have a bit of a kick." He laid the tray on a nearby table and slid into the booth next to Janie. Raising his glass, he toasted, "To us—may we triumph over our enemies."

We touched glasses and drank.

"Okay, how did today's foray go?" Janie asked.

I described my adventure. Janie picked up on the name Darren.

"Wait a minute. That's not—it can't be—"

I nodded. "I really think so."

"What? Who?" Andy looked confused.

"You know Lisa, the woman we met at the dog park? Chester's owner?" Janie reminded him. He nodded. "Her husband is named Darren. Darren Banfield."

"Oh, yeah, him. I remember seeing his name in one of the company newsletters. He's an old friend of the CEO. They golf together or something."

"When we followed Carlie the other evening after work, I thought it looked like Darren Banfield she met. I only saw him walking away though and I wasn't sure."

"Do you think Lisa knows? Is she in on it?"

"I don't know. I hope not, she was kind to me. Well, they both were. But I really hope my disguise fooled her."

Janie shook her head as though to clear it. "Didn't you just want to jump out of that cabinet and confront the pair of them?"

"Actually, all I really wanted at that point was to go back in time and specify a larger cabinet for my new office. My knees thought they were going to die," I confessed.

"How long were you in there?"

"That was the luckiest part of the whole day. As soon as she smashed up those components—which must have taken several days to construct—she went storming out, I guess to lunch. I heard the door slam and then nothing, and when I finally got brave enough to come out, she was gone. And so was her purse. So I went back to the mail room and waited for my heartbeat to return to normal."

"And did we obtain anything useful from her office?"

I shrugged. "In hindsight, we should have planned something to remove her for a longer time. But I did get this." I pulled the North Carolina driver's license out of my pocket and tossed it on the table. "I thought it might be nice to have some ID again."

Janie picked up the plastic square. "This looks awfully real."

"It probably is a real license, though it's not the latest design. My last one, the one that got burned up in my car, had a couple of, I think they call them 'ghost' images of my face on the lower right."

Andy took the card and lightly rubbed his finger over it. "Hmmm. I think..." He picked at the edge. Picked a little more. The top layer of lamination began to loosen. "I wish we had a hair dryer or something to apply some heat."

"Then drink up and let's go to my place," Janie said. "Besides my hair dryer and Jasper's, there are at least seven more in the thrift store."

Andy was right; heat did the trick. The lamination was just clear tape, though it had been very skillfully applied. When he peeled it up, with it came the picture of Fake Beth's face, which had been printed on very thin paper. Below it was the original picture.

Mine.

The name, the number, everything else was part of the original.

"But...I thought your license was destroyed in the car fire," Janie blurted. "How did the imposter get this?"

I stared at the card, loathe to tell them. "I...we...my sister and I..."

"Yes?" Janie's expression was completely sympathetic, so I plunged in.

"We were...I think I told you, we were identical twins. Very, very identical. Not that we had the same personalities, but we did have a very strong connection. And we completely took advantage of being twins. We covered for each other all the time. It probably sounds awful, but we even took classes for each other. It just seemed practical, at least for classes we weren't interested in, those required core courses that no one really wants to take. We split them up and each of us did those classes twice, once in our own name, once in the other's. Damn, this makes us sound as...as conniving as That Woman."

"I wouldn't go that far," Andy said dryly. "I think most of us would have done the same thing if we'd been able to, at least when we were kids."

181

"We probably kept it up longer than we should have, though I hope you'll believe that we stopped a long time ago. But...well, we figured out how to work the system at one point, and we both had driver's licenses in each other's names. Basically we reported we'd lost our licenses and they issued a new one. Not at the same time, of course, a few years apart."

"So this was the license in your name that your sister had?" Janie picked it up again and peered closely at the picture.

"It has to be. And...that means it was among the things that were stolen from her house by the intruder who killed her."

Janie dropped the little plastic rectangle as though her fingertips had been singed. "You mean...this is actual proof of her murder?"

I nodded. "I'd say so."

We all stared at the license, then Andy picked it up and handed it to me. "Put it away. You really should have some identification on you. Janie, can I have a piece of paper? I think we should preserve the overlay. You never know."

She rose and went to her desk, returning with a blank index card. He smoothed the tape with the little picture of Carlie Wilkinson's face onto it and handed it back to Janie, who put it in the desk drawer.

"Okay," he said, "what's next?"

"This can't go on. I'm—I'm tired. I'm tired of being afraid. I—I'm tired of being alone. I never was before. I've either got to confront them, or just give up and go off somewhere and be Mary Claire." I stopped, hating the note in my voice that was too close to a whine.

Janie squared her shoulders. "You're not alone. And it's no choice at all. We're not going to let them get away with this."

"Without my help, I don't thing they will ever succeed with recreating my device. Sooner or later they'll have to give up. The most they'll get away with is my money and belongings. Well, money. I...I don't have much left in the way of belongings." The image of a bombed-out storage unit slid into my mind. I did my best to slide it out again, but it didn't want to go.

Janie started to speak, but Andy stirred. "Ummm, Mary Claire, er, Beth—how much money are we talking about? I know your invention has the potential to make billions, but, well, how much are you worth?"

A couple of eons passed as I did some figuring in my head. "When they got control...about seven million. Could be more. Or less. I hadn't looked at it recently."

Janie blinked. Andy whistled.

"That alone is motive for them to steal your life," he said. "Of course, the payoff from your rain-maker will make seven million look like chump change. I can't see them ever giving up until they have you in their control."

"It's not just the money," Janie argued. "They stole your *name*. Your reputation, your past. Your future. It's a lot of money, but in the end it's only money. *You* lose millions and it is exactly the same as someone who only has a quarter losing that quarter. But your name...no. They cannot have that. And I have an idea."

20

"Hello, Valerie? Hi, it's Andy from the mail room...Good, thanks, but...no, no, but I am afraid we have a bit of a situation. Could you come up to the fifth floor...Right. Now if you possibly can...That new woman's office...Right, Dr. Harding...Thanks. Oh, and I think you won't want to tell anyone where you're going...Great. See you in a minute."

Andy dropped the receiver into its cradle on the desk phone and looked at me with a raised eyebrow and half-smile. "*Doctor* Harding? You're a doctor?"

I shrugged.

"Medical or PhD?"

"PhD."

"May I ask where from? Just curious."

"Found it in a Cracker Jack box."

"Come on. Tell me."

"Stanford."

"And I thought my puny little BA from Willamette made me a tad over-educated for the mail room."

"I'm just good at taking tests."

"You're good at something. I looked up your patents, you know."

I glared at him. "Who said you could do that?"

"I did. I couldn't even figure out what the hell some of them are for."

"Yeah, well, a lot of screwy inventions get patented. The patent office is full of them."

He shook his head, the smile getting broader. "I hope I get to know you long enough and well enough to get to the bottom of your secrets."

"Oh, Andy, you may already know too many." I tried to match his smile. "At this point, I just hope we make it through today."

A discreet knock sounded on the closed door. Andy quickly stepped over to it and pulled it open an inch, peering through the gap, then stepped back to admit Valerie. Very quickly her expression changed from inquisitive to appalled as she surveyed the room.

"What the—what the hell is going on?" Valerie sputtered.

"I know, I know," Andy said. "We found her like this."

"I knew there was something off about the woman but—"

"Oh, you noticed it too?" Andy flicked me a glance where I stood quietly by the window.

186

"—but this is just disgraceful. Good god, it's only ten-thirty in the morning!"

'I know. Unbelievable."

"Not that this would be excusable any time of day." She crossed her arms over her body and glared at the figure slumped over the desk. "All right, give me a minute to think what's best to do." Her eyes roamed around the room as though searching for an answer. "Oh, Mary Claire, I didn't even see you there. I'm sorry."

I looked at the floor. "That's okay, Mrs. Frost."

I put my hands in the pocket of the horizontally-striped cardigan that Janie had issued to me from the thrift store, feeling the slightly damp cloth I had stashed there.

Valerie spoke again. "Obviously, we can't let anyone see her like this. There may be some legitimate explanation. Other than the obvious one, I mean."

Andy nodded. "True, though I'd be pretty surprised. I do have a suggestion."

"Yes?"

"You might want to document the situation with a couple of pictures. I mean, most people would deny something like this, and if you need to take, um, disciplinary action, then it wouldn't be just her word against yours."

"Oh, right. Hmmm. I'm not completely sure of the legalities here, but—okay, just a couple. I'll keep them on my phone and not do anything with them unless I have to."

She pulled out a smart phone and proceeded to take at least half a dozen shots from several directions.

"There, that should do. Did either of you try to wake her?"

"I—I did," I chirped. "As soon as I found her like this. I mean, all I did was say her name and then I touched her on the shoulder. I...didn't want to make her mad or anything."

All of this was true, except that I'd actually given her a rough shake while saying her name—her real name—quite loudly close to her ear. I had to make sure the chloroform had worked sufficiently. She was definitely out for the count.

Valerie moved closer to the figure slumped in the desk chair and with an expression of distaste, leaned close and sniffed. Then she reared back, fanning her nose. "Ewww, she smells like a distillery."

The smell actually emanated from the pool of Scotch that Andy had poured onto the desk blotter before lowering the Fake Beth's cheek onto it. More scent wafted from the crystal glass by her hand that had about an inch of booze in it. The almost empty bottle of Macallan lay on its side near the corner of the desk. The bottle cap was on the floor.

Still with wrinkled nose, Valerie leaned close to Fake Beth. "Dr. Harding, wake up. Dr. Harding?" With two fingers she poked her shoulder.

Fake Beth emitted something close to a snort.

"Okay, I can think of two options." Valerie straightened. Her voice became authoritative. "We could just leave her here. Let her sleep it off. Pretend nothing happened."

"Do you—do you think that's, um, safe?" I offered timidly.

"What do you mean, dear?"

"Well, what if there's a fire? Or—or an earthquake or something?"

Andy nodded. "Or she might choke on her own spit and die. You hear about stuff like that."

I shot him a look. He sounded far too enthusiastic.

"Yes, I suppose you're right. We could end up with some horrible tragedy on our hands, although...er, never mind. I guess one of you could stay with her until she awakens. Another possibility is to get her out of here, take her home, and let her sleep it off there."

"That certainly sounds like the best plan." Andy's smile was genuine. Valerie was following her script perfectly, even though she was unaware he'd written it for her.

"But how can we get her out of the building? Discreetly, I mean."

"I see what you mean. Guess I can't just throw her over my shoulder in a fireman's lift and cart her out. Oh, wait, that's it!"

"What's it? You could hurt yourself doing something like that. And what if you dropped her? Plus, we'd never get her out without half the building knowing about it. The first person who saw you would call five others and by the time we reached the lobby it would be like standing room only on the viewing stand for the Rose Parade."

"No, no, I said cart. We have the perfect cart in the mail room, a big flatbed thing I use for large deliveries. I even have a bunch of moving pads. We could put a couple under her and then cover her up with more and it would look like I was just taking the pads somewhere."

Valerie's expression had changed to hopeful. "I think that might work. Well done, Andy." She looked over the snoring figure slumped on the desk consideringly. "Do you think the three of us could move her onto it? And off again. Oh dear, you have a motorcycle, you can hardly take her home on that."

"I have a car," I offered. "Could we put her in the back seat?"

Andy snapped his fingers. "The company van. I can bring it into the loading area, we'll make sure the coast is clear, and then lift her into the cargo area. If we pack some of the pads around her she shouldn't roll around too much."

"But how would you get her into the house? Perhaps if I come along, the three of us could carry her in. I have an important meeting in a little while, but I suppose I could reschedule it."

This was something we had not anticipated. I could see how Valerie had ended up with eleven cats and the famous three-legged iguana.

"Do you think she would have a desk chair at home?" I said. "We could put her in it and roll her in. Kind of like a wheel chair. I'm sure Andy and I could do that."

Valerie nodded slowly. Andy pressed on.

190

"No one will notice if Mary Claire and I are gone for a while, but someone would be bound to miss you. I mean, of course you could explain your absence if you had to, but, well…"

"You're right, the whole point is to be discreet."

Fake Beth gave an especially loud snore and smacked her lips. Valerie straightened.

"All right, that's what we'll do. Andy, go get the cart and the blankets."

"You bet. Mary Claire, come with me and you can move the van into place so we don't waste any time once we get her down there."

"I'll tidy up in here a bit while I'm waiting," Valerie offered. "Oh, Andy, bring along a box of some kind. I think I should, um, preserve the evidence." She picked up the liquor bottle and squinted at the label. "Huh. Forty-year-old Macallan single malt. This is pretty pricey stuff to be knocking back at work." After a short pause she added, "Too damn bad she drank it all."

21

Andy and I stared down at the unconscious figure in the old black leather office chair, the one I had loaded onto a moving van a lifetime ago. She looked amazingly normal, just a middle-aged woman dressed in a short, tight skirt, white silk blouse and red high heels who had fallen asleep in a chair.

The rope tied around her did add a bit of an incongruous note.

He leaned forward and tested her bonds. "Tight enough, but probably won't cut off the circulation. Too much. Will you be okay here alone with her until I get back?"

"Sure. You get the van back to the office." I didn't add that I couldn't guarantee how okay *she* would be. She'd just better not wake up while I was alone with her. I didn't think I would do anything to her while she slept, but awake…no promises.

"Okay. I'll get back as soon as I can."

"Oh, here are the keys for Jasper's car." I had picked up Andy that morning and we'd ridden to work together so that he wouldn't have to worry about his bike.

"Call Janie right away."

"I will. Don't worry."

I walked with him through the house, silent and still empty except for the bedroom with the furniture and boxes from my moving van. We had come by early that morning and made sure that no one had discovered the broken glass back in the master bedroom. Fake Beth's "home address" was exactly as I had left it on my last visit. It seemed like a good omen when we found a remote control for the door opener out in the attached garage.

He climbed into the van, and I pressed the doorbell-like button on the door frame. The garage door slid up. He sketched a little wave, backed the van out, aimed the remote, and drove away as the door rumbled shut. I stood leaning on the doorway, staring blankly into the empty garage. An unknown amount of time later my eyes came back into focus and I registered the shining bits of dust floating through shafts of sunlight that slanted in through the high row of windows in the garage door.

I pulled the phone from my pocket and dialed.

"Good afternoon, Pick of the Litter Thrift Store."

"Janie, it's me."

"Beth! Where are you? How did it go?"

"I'm at the house. Andy just left to take the van back."

"And she's—she's there?"

"Oh yes."

"It worked?"

"Like a charm. She saw the Ooshy Gooshy Bar on the desk and picked it right up, no questions asked. As soon as she started to unwrap it I snuck up behind her with the chloroform. And then she was sound asleep."

"I can't believe you had the nerve to do that."

"I surprised myself. Probably a good thing Andy was there though, to make sure I didn't leave the cloth on her face too long. Anyway, there's no need for you to rush over here, she'll be asleep for a while yet. And she's tied up good and tight. But when you do come…"

"Yes? What do you need?"

"Bring Clover along, would you?"

"Are you sure? She won't be in the way?"

"I'm sure." I paused, then added, "I might be able to kill that woman in front of you, but I don't think I could kill her in front of my dog."

"Maybe I'd better come over there soon."

"Yeah. Maybe you should."

"Weird." Janie put her hands on her hips and pursed her lips as she stared down at the snoring figure, incongruous in the empty kitchen.

"What?" I looked up from my whispered conversation with Clover.

194

"Well, this is the first time I've seen her. I guess I was expecting something more, I don't know, more overtly evil. She just looks like a person."

"I know. That may be the scariest thing of all. You can't tell a thing by looking at someone."

"Do you really think that's true? I mean, I know we can all be fooled sometimes..."

"I—I don't know. I used to think I could assess character, at least well enough for everyday purposes. But after everything that has happened, I really do not know. I'm not sure I'll ever be able to trust my judgment again."

She laid a hand on my shoulder. "Everyone feels that way when they've been betrayed. Or victimized. But it has nothing to do with you or your ability to judge character. Their actions are *their* actions."

"I know. I do, really. I just hope—I'm not entirely sure what *my* actions are going to be now."

"They will be in keeping with your character. Which I actually know a lot about."

"Oh yeah?"

"Of course. I've seen you with your dog."

I gave a little laugh. "You have at that. And honestly, knowing what you do about her—" I waved my hand at the slumped figure in the chair—"could you imagine her having a dog?"

"Never in a million years. You know, I think we should move her."

"What, like roll her up and down the hall for fun? I guess it would pass the time until she wakes up."

"You have the oddest ideas. No, what I was actually thinking was, let's move her to some other room and leave her facing a wall or something so she can't see much when she wakes up. It might, I don't know, help keep her off balance."

"Okay, sure. The master bedroom is probably the quietest room in the house."

One of the chair wheels squeaked as we pushed Fake Beth down the hall. It was such a familiar sound that I felt a little dizzy. It had squeaked for months back in North Carolina, and every time I heard it I would think I should get the oil. And every time as soon as I stood up I forgot.

When we reached our destination, Janie looked around the room. "Oooh, the closet, even better. We don't have to close the door, but if we put her in that corner she won't be able to see much at all."

"Are you sure we can't spin her around a few times just for fun?"

Janie shook her head. "Hell no, she'd probably puke. Let me just get her into place, and then you and I are going to occupy our time in the other bedroom. Where your stuff is."

I backed a couple of steps away. "I'd really rather not. It feels so...tainted."

She shoved the chair into the closet, then turned back to me. "I know. We had burglars break into our house once and they went through everything. But everything. I made my husband throw away all my underwear that they had pawed through. I just couldn't touch it."

"Exactly."

"You won't have to do anything but sit there. But come with me. There might be stuff I need to ask you what you want done with."

"Well..."

"I can't just stand around and look at a horrible person snoring in a chair in a closet. Look, this house belongs to someone, and they shouldn't have to deal with your abandoned property once the lease runs out." She walked over to me and took my wrist in her hand. "Come on. You sit there with Clover, and I'll put stuff back into boxes. If you want, everything can go to the thrift store. We'll sell it for a pittance and use the money to feed homeless puppies. Something good can come from something bad."

I nodded. Before I followed her, I pulled off the stretched-out cardigan that was a mainstay of Mary Claire's look and draped it over Carlie's head. I wanted her to be as disoriented as possible. Then I left the master bedroom, pulling the door shut behind me.

When I reached the front bedroom, I sank into a corner. Clover crawled into my lap and curled up into her thirty-pound-river-stone guise. As all the blood circulation to my feet slowly ceased, I watched Janie sort through the detritus of my old life, shoving torn and broken items into a large black garbage bag she had brought, re-boxing the rest. I wondered if I would ever own anything again. The only time I spoke was when I saw Janie pull a long chef's knife out of a box, along with the sharpening steel that Georgette had given me three birthdays ago.

197

"Janie? Let me—let me have those. We might need something to cut her ropes off eventually."

I laid the knife beside me on the floor, and wondered how one can deal with a monster without becoming a monster oneself.

Andy returned earlier than I expected, carrying a large stainless steel bowl. He headed for the kitchen. Filling the bowl with water, he explained, "Just in case Clover didn't bring her water bowl."

"We did forget it," I confessed. "But how did you know she would be here?"

"Just a hunch."

"What are you doing back here so soon?"

"Valerie told me to get out whatever mail was ready to go. She said to drop off the bags at the PO and then come back here."

"So she didn't say anything about my not coming back to work?" I asked.

"I called her as soon as I got back to let her know we had delivered 'Dr. Harding' safe and sound to her home. I said you volunteered to stay and make sure she continued to be all right, and that I would pick you up after work. That's when she told me to go ahead and come back over here."

"She also said—" his voice changed to Valerie's exact intonations—"I think we got *very* lucky with Mary Claire. She is just a find.' Janie, she's going to call you and thank you for sending Mary Claire to her."

"And so she should." Janie gave a single, emphatic nod. "She ought to do more than—"

Clover's ears cocked and she shot out of the room. From the other end of the house came a muffled groan. The three of us looked at each other.

"It's show time," I said. I stood up from my corner, surreptitiously picking up the knife and steel. Andy led the way into the hall and started toward the master bedroom.

22

"Wait!" I hissed at my companions. I beckoned them away from the door. I whispered, "Let her think it's just me here with her."

Our prisoner was audibly showing signs of life. "Hey! Let me out! Help!"

Andy scowled. "But what if—"

"Shhhh. I might get more out of her if she believes it's just the two of us. You know, if she thinks there aren't any witnesses. Keep Clover here with you."

They looked at each other, then nodded. I snapped my fingers and Clover ceased sniffing at the door at the end of the hall and came running. Janie took hold of her collar and whispered, "Be careful. Good luck. We'll be right outside the door if you need us."

I quietly entered the room, any sound made by my footsteps covered by the noise our prisoner made. The afternoon light shone now on the other side of the house, and this dimly lit room felt sad and empty, the carpet a little damp, the short draperies over the windows hanging a bit crooked. The figure tied to the chair in the closet was the perfect decorative touch.

Fake Beth shook her head, trying to dislodge the sweater, but to no avail. She yelled again in a rusty voice, "Help! Help! Can anyone hear me? Help!"

I crept up behind her and spun the chair one hundred eighty degrees so she was facing me. She uttered a little yelp. After a moment I pulled the sweater off of her head. She blinked, swallowed. Squinted at me.

"What the...Who are you? Let me loose, damn it!"

I stared down at her. The wig that turned me into Mary Claire had never felt tighter.

"I don't know who the hell you are, but you can't do this. Untie me at once." She seemed to be aiming for a note of authority, but it came out as petulance. I said nothing.

"Wait a minute. I've seen you somewhere." She stared at my face. Swallowed. "What the hell is this? Who *are* you? What is going on? Untie me, do you hear?"

I kept looking at her. A feeling of power grew in me with every heartbeat.

"You'd better untie me, you bitch. You'll never get away with this." No trace of her assumed accent.

I remained silent. She stared back. After a minute that felt like a week I saw a tremble in her lower lip, but her voice maintained its sneer.

"Let. Me. Go. Now, I tell you. You're going to be sorry. I know I've seen you somewhere. I *will* be able to tell the police who you are."

I let my silence spin out a little longer. When I spoke in Mary Claire's Boston voice, I was surprised at how gently the words came out.

"I'm standing right in front of you, and you don't even know who I am."

That's when the first flicker of fear flitted across her eyes. I smiled at her.

"But hey, you're Doctor Beth Harding, aren't you? You're an intelligent woman. Come on, I bet you can figure out where you've seen my face before."

I could almost see the wheels spinning in her brain as she tried to work it out.

"You...are you...I know, you're that girl who—"

"Girl? Oh, come now. I'm older than you by a year or so. Do you still think of yourself as a girl?" I looked pointedly at her shoes. "Maybe you do at that."

The memory clicked into place. "I've seen you at work. The—the delivery person. Something like that."

"That's right, Carlie." I let my voice find its normal accent. "I'm from the mail room."

I could see her eyes widen as she realized what name I had used. Before she could speak she had to gulp.

"That's not...I'm not..."

"And I'm not Mary Claire Johnson, the mail room clerk." I reached up with my left hand and pulled off the wig. I could feel my own hair standing every which way, but I left it in disarray. I dropped Mary Claire's posture along with the wig.

She stared up at me, licked her lips. She looked pale, even a bit green, like grocery store lettuce well past its sell-by date.

"I—I have no idea who you are."

"Oh, come on, Carlie. Don't bore me with these stupid games. We are way, way past that."

"You're crazy. I don't know what you're talking about. Untie me. Right now, do you hear?"

"Actually, I can't untie you."

"Of course you can."

"No. Really. I tied those ropes very, very tight. They'll have to be cut off with a knife. And Carlie," I paused to give her a half-smile, "you do not want me close to you with this knife."

I held up the chef's knife. Her eyes grew wide. That might have been the first moment she fully realized the depth of her predicament.

I kept my voice even, almost hypnotic. "Because I really cannot trust myself, Carlie. I have a feeling that the ropes might not be the only thing that would get cut. A knife can slip, you know. Accidentally. Accidents can happen to anyone. Accidents like car brakes failing, or an ATM eating a debit card. Or a bomb in a storage unit. Or even in an empty house."

She sucked in her breath, but didn't say anything. In a moment I went on.

"Accidents can very easily happen to people who are tied tightly to a chair, alone in an empty house.

Well, alone except for the one person in the world you have harmed the most."

I let my smile grow wide. No doubt I looked as crazed as I felt. She gulped. "You wouldn't."

"Yes, I think I would. But for now, for this minute, you're safe." I laid the knife and steel down on the floor and held up my empty hands. "No knife."

She could not hide her relief. I let her feel it for a few seconds. "They say all we have is the present moment, and in this moment you're still all right. Nothing really bad has happened to you. But it was terribly thoughtful of you to leave all my stuff in the other room when you emptied out my moving van. Remember that box of kitchen utensils? I'm quite a good cook, Carlie, and I appreciate good equipment."

I paused to let her imagination run amok.

"Good equipment...for instance, very...sharp...knives."

I bent and picked up the two items on the floor, and drew the blade slowly across the steel. The soft rasping sound somehow filled the room.

She shivered. "Stop it. Just stop it!"

"So now we know where we are. In the present moment, you're still okay. But things change. I never realized I was capable of hurting someone, but I believe I just might be. If I did decide to go that route, how long do you think I should make it last? The hurting, I mean."

She swayed in the chair. The ropes were the only thing keeping her from falling.

"I suppose the punishment *should* fit the crime. How long have you been pretending to be me here in Salem? A couple of weeks? No, that would be too long. Well, not too long for your crimes, but I don't think I could keep you alive for two weeks once you started bleeding."

I heard a little noise from the doorway and glanced over there. Janie and Andy stared at me, their eyes wide. Andy's mouth hung open. Clover, her collar still held by Janie, cocked her head questioningly.

Good. They would stop me before I went too far. I was almost as relieved as Carlie would have been if she'd known. But her sight lines were still limited by the side wall of the closet; as far as she knew it was just the two of us. I brought my eyes back to her face.

"So how about a couple of days, Carlie? I wonder if you could bleed for a couple of days. That's how long my sister was in a hospital bed, blood seeping into her brain. Before she died."

I pulled the blade of the knife across the steel again. And again. She began to twist and struggle against her bonds. "Let me go! You're crazy!"

I nodded. "You could be right. You could be very, very right." I felt the blade with the ball of my thumb, considered it thoughtfully, then gave it another strop.

She strove for a few seconds more. I held my breath. Would the knots hold? When she gave up and was still, I eased out a breath. Neither Andy nor I had ever tied anyone up before.

"You really should not have kept that driver's license." I forced my voice to stay even. "You do realize it places you at my sister's murder, right?"

"No! I wasn't...I didn't...it wasn't me!"

"Right. Of course not. You just happened to paste your picture on a driver's license that was stolen from her house. Stolen during the robbery where she was killed."

"It *wasn't*...that wasn't the plan." She renewed her struggle. "It was an accident!"

Blood rushed to my face. Even to my eyeballs, because suddenly I was looking at her through a red haze. "An accident? You hit her so hard with that piece of firewood that it killed her...by *accident*?"

My hands curled tighter around the handle of the knife and I took one step toward her.

"No! Yes! Keep away from me. He didn't mean to do it."

I took one more step in her direction.

"She grabbed the piece of wood and started swinging. He—he wrestled it from her. She wouldn't stop screaming. He didn't mean—"

"*Shut up, Carlie!*"

The new voice cut through hers at the same moment Andy and Janie catapulted into the room. Carlie shrieked. I had to gulp back my own scream when I saw Darren Banfield right behind them, the black fury in his eyes matched by the cold eye of the gun he pointed at us.

23

"All right, get out."

I stumbled as I slid out of the back seat of the SUV. It was difficult to keep my balance with my hands tied behind me. I caught myself before I fell on my knees, reeling a few steps. Clover jumped out of the car and followed me.

"Stay with me, sweetheart," I murmured to her, then turned back to see how Janie and Andy were faring. Janie was standing by the black vehicle, looking around the forest clearing in which we were parked. As I watched, Andy slid across the leather seat and hopped out, stumbling as I had.

Late afternoon sun slanted through the branches of the firs. The air smelled clean and fresh, almost herbal. Dust still hung in the air over the narrow logging road we had followed from the highway, but it would soon settle and there would be nothing to indicate where we had gone.

Darren pointed with his gun. "Up that trail."

Carlie looked at the trail, then back at Darren in disbelief. "Are you nuts? I'm wearing four inch heels."

His voice was clipped. "I need you to help keep them in line. So either walk in those heels or go barefoot."

She opted to keep her shoes on. I was glad Mary Claire had put on sensible walking shoes that morning.

"All right, let's go. And no funny business."

My unruly brain hared off with the phrase "funny business." Slapstick, I thought. We could do pratfalls to confuse them. No, we'd never be able to get up again with our hands tied like this. I settled for imagining a Monty Python-style silly walk that I could do and still maintain my balance.

Andy was in the lead, Carlie at his heels, struggling to walk on the forest trail in her heels. Darren had given her a pistol, but she kept forgetting to point it in Andy's direction. She handled a gun almost as well as she did an accent. Not the person I myself would have partnered with for a criminal enterprise. What confluence of events could have brought her and Darren together?

Janie was behind her, then me. I had no illusions that Darren was as lax with his gun. There was a particular spot between my shoulders blades that felt very cold.

The trail led steadily upward. Even though it wasn't terribly steep, it was hard to climb without the use of my arms. Clover stayed close, though she couldn't help dropping her nose to the ground from time to time. "Good girl," I whispered to her. "Stay with me. Don't go near Darren."

I looked at Janie's back. She seemed to be twitching slightly as she walked. I had been puzzled and a little irritated by her, back at the house. Darren and his gun had taken all of us by surprise, and he had no trouble herding us into a corner and keeping us covered while he sawed through Carlie's bonds with the knife I had dropped in my surprise. Once she was loose, she tottered to her feet and tried to throw her arms around him, but he shook her off roughly.

"Oh, Darren, thank god you're here." Her words came out somewhere between a sob and a whine. He kept his eyes on us as he held out the knife to her.

"Here. Cut that rope into pieces and then tie up their wrists."

She took the knife and clumsily sawed three sections of rope off the longest piece. When she approached us I tensed, thinking I could seize her and use her as a hostage. But Darren read my mind.

"Hold it," he barked. "Don't let any of them grab you. One at a time. Move into the middle of the room."

Janie immediately stepped forward with her hands held out in front of her. Tears dripped off her face. She looked beaten and humble.

Carlie reached toward her with a piece of rope.

"Not like that, you idiot!" His tone was scathing. "Tie her hands behind her. Jesus."

Janie half turned and proffered her wrists once more, this time in back. Carlie tied them together,

209

biting her lip as she did so. She looked ready to join Janie in producing tears. Then Janie backed away from her, returning to our corner, never taking her stricken gaze off Darren.

Andy was next, then it was my turn. By now Carlie had her hands under control, and I could feel the relish with which she cinched the tightest knots she could manage around my wrists.

Now, walking up a narrow trail through some of the tallest trees I'd ever seen, I focused on Janie's hands. Suddenly I realized what the small twitches were about.

She was working on escaping from her bonds. I could see that the circle of rope around her wrists was looser than mine.

I did my best to recall how she had been positioned when she was tied. She was mostly turned away from Darren, and the way she held her hands together behind her...of course. She had been as meek as milk, obviously crying, putting up absolutely no resistance—and had turned her hands parallel to her back, thumbs together. Carlie might have tied them tightly, but now Janie had turned her hands so the palms faced each other.

And the tight rope was no longer tight.

I did what I could to shield her from Darren's sight. I was both taller and broader than she, and I walked as close to her as possible without stepping on her heels. I wasn't sure what she could do if she did manage to get loose, but it had to be more than any of could accomplish while we were tied.

"Where are you taking us, anyway?" I asked loudly. Focus on me, I thought. Do not look at Janie.

"Shut up." Gone was the charming man at whose table I had eaten macaroni and cheese. Whose dog I had enjoyed at the dog park. I thought back to the conversation Janie and I had had...when? An hour ago? A lifetime?...about how we couldn't imagine the Fake Beth having a dog. And now her accomplice was behind me with a gun, and he lived with one of the nicest dogs I had ever met.

Chester would be so ashamed of him.

I could not think of anything more damning.

"Look, walking uphill with my hands tied is really hard." Telling me to shut up rarely has the effect the speaker desires. I glanced over my shoulder at Darren. "I'd just like to know how much longer I have to do this."

His answering smirk was so full of satisfaction that I had to look away. "Not much further. But you're probably going to wish we'd kept going."

The trail became a little steeper. We climbed a little slower. I didn't know what our elevation was; my shortness of breath was probably due not to lack of oxygen from being high on a mountain but more to the climb. And being afraid.

A large blue bird with a dark hooded crest flashed by, landing on a nearby branch. It gave a raucous jay's scream, hopped to another branch, flew away.

I began to hear a noise ahead. It made me think of those white noise generators people use to help them sleep. In a few more minutes we came out into a clearing where the noise was louder. Sunlight filtered through the boughs of the surrounding firs, striping the ground with the shadows of their trunks.

"Stop here," Darren commanded.

Everyone halted. We all turned to face him. Janie edged a bit behind me, her shoulder touching my arm. I could feel the little movements in her muscles as she continued to work at her rope. Clover ran up, tongue lolling, and threw herself down on my feet. She looked up at me with that little squint dogs use to tell you they love you. I gazed into her amber eyes and felt love and dread in equal amounts.

It could not be a good thing for a man with a gun and the woman who had been successfully impersonating me to bring us to a remote spot in the woods. The breeze that stirred the branches of the firs ever so slightly suddenly felt much, much colder.

"And now," Darren announced, a smug smile curving up the corners of his lips, "we are going to have a little conversation."

24

Buy time. It was the only thought my mind could focus on. I didn't really think we were going to walk back down the hill again, but as I had pontificated earlier to Carlie, for just this moment we were okay.

Modo liceat vivere, est spes.

While there's life, there's hope.

So when Darren announced with a smile that we were going to converse, I decided to go for it.

"Oh, yes?" I said brightly. "And what would you like to converse about? Let's see, we could do bird watching, that large blue thing that just flew by is unfamiliar to me. Of course since I'm new to Oregon, you could make up anything and I wouldn't know the difference. Ditto with the trees. I don't think I've seen any loblolly pines on our nature hike today, so those are probably just east coast trees. I think our forests

213

in North Carolina also lean toward more deciduous varieties. Have you ever flown to Raleigh or Atlanta in the spring? The dogwoods blooming below the bigger trees are quite a stunning sight. Or how about books or movies? That new—"

The barrel of Darren's gun focused its evil eye on me.

"Shut the fuck up."

"Well, you did say—"

He took two steps toward me. I felt the vibration of Clover's growl through my shoe, but it wasn't audible.

"Good girl," I told her softly. "Stay."

"There's only one thing we have to discuss. Where are the rest of the plans for the rain maker?"

I blinked in confusion and turned toward Andy, managing to partially hide Janie as I did. "Rain maker? Andy, do you know what he's talking about?"

He shook his head. "No, I have no idea. A rain maker? Like a shaman, you mean?" He looked Darren in the eyes, ignoring the gun.

Darren's face was getting red. "Jesus, you people are like some comedy troupe. Cut the Laurel and Hardy crap."

Ah hah, I thought. I should have gone with the slapstick idea earlier. Maybe we could have finished with this confrontation without having to hike up a mountain. I tuned back in to Darren.

"...and we know you didn't send all the files to WETCo. Believe me, we'd have found them by now.

They must exist somewhere. Tell me where they are so we can all go home."

I couldn't help it. I laughed out loud.

"What?" he scowled in return.

"Why on earth would you assume those files—if there ever were such files—would still exist?"

"You promised the complete project to Martin Linder."

"Ahhh, there's the confusion. I did contract with Mr. Linder for the complete project. However, I did not offer him the *completed* project, which appears to be what you are after. The project is still in development. My, er, doppelganger over there can verify that."

Carlie had evidently gotten bored. She still had the gun Darren had given her, but she held it loosely and pointed at the ground. She paced in a little circle behind Andy. The ground was rocky and she wobbled in her ridiculous shoes.

Darren noticed her the same time I did.

"Carlie!" he barked. She started and looked at him. I thought there might be a little fear on her face. "Watch what you're doing, you stupid bitch. You'll go over."

She looked around, then jumped back toward our little group. "Oh my god! Why didn't you tell me I was standing on the edge of a cliff?"

"I thought you might have the sense to notice."

I suddenly realized what the white noise I'd been hearing must be. We were four feet from a cliff—and at its base was a rushing river.

The knowledge made our situation seem much, much worse.

With an effort I pulled my attention back to Darren. He was for the moment focused on his partner in crime. I shifted my weight so that I was a little more in front of Janie. She took a tiny sideways step to place herself more behind me. Neither of our captors seemed to notice, though I was pretty sure Andy did.

Darren frowned. "Carlie, pay attention. In spite of what this idiot you replaced seems to think, this is not a nature hike. You have a gun. Point it at one of them." He pulled his gaze back to me. "And as for you, I've had enough. Where are the plans?"

I had had enough too. "Did it never occur to you that blowing up—or burning up—everything I own might not be a good idea?" I loaded my voice with the most scathing sarcasm I was capable of. "Those plans? You. Blew. Them. Up."

He stared at me. His eyes flickered back and forth as he considered what I'd said. "No. I don't believe you."

"Believe it. You put the project back years. *Years.* I doubt now if it will ever be completed in our lifetimes."

"Impossible. Linder said you were close, he wanted me to find capital investors for production."

"I do admire his optimism. Even before you started bombing storage units and sabotaging brakes—that was you, wasn't it?—there was still a lot of work to be done."

"I want those plans. Now."

"And I cannot give them to you. You are hoist on your own petard, whatever the hell a petard is. *You blew up the plans.*"

He was starting to believe me. I saw the eye of the gun move a little, as though his hand had the smallest of tremors. "No. No. You're lying. Carlie was sure you had them."

"Oh, for god's sake. You believed *her?*"

"She knew what she was talking about. She said she's followed your career for years. Since college. You and your sister."

"Ah, yes, college. Did she tell you about her own college career?"

"She went to MIT. Just like you."

I glanced over at Carlie. Her expression was blank, as though she didn't realize we were discussing her. "Not exactly like me. Us. My twin and I actually graduated." I raised my voice a little. "Did you tell him what you did, Carlie?"

She focused on me. Her lips tightened into a little prune of a mouth.

"What?" Darren looked rapidly back and forth from me to her.

"It's true that she *went* to MIT. But it's also true that they expelled her for cheating. I never knew the details, I didn't care. But why would she cheat unless she couldn't do the work?"

"Shut up!" Carlie closed the gap between us and shoved the gun into my stomach. "Just shut up. You have no idea what it was like."

I thought that this might be the time I actually should shut up. I didn't know if a point blank stomach shot would immediately kill me, but even if it didn't I would bleed to death before I could get off this mountain.

"You and your sister...always together, no one could tell you apart. You were so fucking smart. Everything was easy for you. And you never had to do anything to be noticed. Everyone knew who you were, just because there were two of you."

How we had hated that attention, Georgette and I. No matter how low-key we tried to be, how hard we worked at blending in, we were always singled out. Just because we looked alike. We were smart, and creative, and diligent, but the only thing the world seemed to value was that we looked alike.

I suddenly realized that what we had most hated, being conspicuous, always being the center of attention, was what Carlie had craved the most.

I looked at her tear-stained face, so close to my own. The day had not been kind to the makeup she had applied that morning. Most of it was gone, with only some mascara left to smear under her eyes. Her hair was a tangled mess.

She had taken so much from me. Home, job, money, possessions. Sister.

And I had not even been able to remember her name.

25

"Carlie! Stop it!"

I saw her flinch at the anger in Darren's voice. She stood so close I could feel the exact moment she gave up. Slowly the pressure of the gun lessened as she turned toward him. The breath I had not been able to expel from my lungs was released.

For just this moment, everything was all right.

"Damn it, we still need her. We have to get those plans."

She took two steps toward him. Her voice was low. "You said you needed me."

He didn't hear her. Or pretended not to. He motioned with the gun. "Move back where you were, you're in the way."

"You said you needed me." A little louder. Another step.

He looked past her, or through her, at me. "This is your last chance. Where are the plans? Believe me, you're going to produce them one way or another. If you don't tell me where they are, I'll lock you up until you produce new ones. Don't tell me you don't have them in your head."

My voice was almost as low as Carlie's. "That is exactly what I am telling you. And do you know why? Because *you killed the wrong twin.*"

Everything stopped. Behind me Janie's micro movements stilled. Carlie paused with one foot in front of the other. Andy pulled in a deep breath and held it. Clover gazed at me unblinkingly. Darren stared. It was exactly like one of those movie scenes where everyone is frozen except the hero, who has stepped out of time and can move freely among them.

And then Darren blinked. I practically spat the words at him.

"You killed the wrong twin. You're right, Beth could have produced the plans again. In her sleep. Standing on her head. But you killed her."

"But—but you're Beth."

"No."

"You must be." He seemed unaware when Carlie began to move like a sleepwalker toward him again. She might have been invisible for all the attention he paid to her.

"I wish I were. But I'm no more Beth than she is." I tilted my head in Carlie's direction. Still his focus remained entirely on me. We might have been alone in a tunnel, just the two of us. The hand holding the gun began to tremble in earnest.

"It was the other sister's house. She was there alone. Georgette. It was her house."

"It was my house. Beth was there. We'd been working and I ran into town to pick up lunch."

The word lunch seemed to hit him with the force of a blow.

Carlie moved the last step to close the distance between them. She found her voice.

"You said you needed ME! I did...all this...because you needed me. Loved...*me.*" She raised the hand holding the gun and swung at him.

He batted her away as though she were an annoying fly, not even looking at her. She reeled backwards, spun, and the high heel of her left shoe caught on a rock. She pitched forward in a sprawl, a cry of anguish escaping her.

Her gun skittered forward, straight toward me. Janie leapt out from behind me and dove for it, hands reaching. Grabbed it. Rolled into a sitting position, arms outstretched, left hand supporting the weight of the gun in her right.

"Drop the gun, Darren."

He laughed. "Yeah, right. Like you really have the guts to shoot me."

"I'm not going to start with you. I'm going to start with her." All of the disgust Janie felt for the woman who had impersonated me landed on that last word.

From the corner of my eye I caught the swivel of Andy's head as he stared at her. In front of me Darren's smile got wider, a full set of crocodile teeth.

"Go ahead. I don't care. All I want is the rain maker. And the power that comes with it. In fact..."

Quite casually, he aimed the gun at Carlie where she still lay sprawled on the rocky ground. And shot her. Janie's gun fell from her hand and lay on the ground between us.

Clover yelped at the noise and skittered away. I wanted to call her, tell her everything was okay, but I was frozen.

Darren dropped to one knee, gun aimed at me again. He patted his thigh and in a crooning voice called, "It's okay, girl, come on. Clover, come."

She gave a tentative wag and took a step toward him. I tried to yell at her, tell her no, but my throat was paralyzed.

"That's a good girl. Come on."

We had eaten at his table. He had fed her treats at the dog park. She went to him, head down, and he scooped her up under his left arm. Stood. I saw the tip of her sweet whippy tail move back and forth as she looked at his face.

Making a wide circle around us, Darren carried Clover to the edge of the precipice.

"Now give me the plans, or the dog goes in the river."

26

"No! Don't!" My knees unlocked and I tottered toward the man holding my dog.

He made a move toward the edge, and I stopped. "No, please, no. Let her go." I didn't care that I was begging.

"All of you, sit on the ground. You—" he pointed at Janie with his pistol— "push the gun this way with your foot."

We all obeyed. I don't think my legs would have held me up any longer anyway. I sank down on my knees, then onto my butt next to Janie. A sharp rock jabbed my hip. I let it. Andy was close to Janie's other side. A few feet away, Carlie's body was as still as a fallen forest log. One shoe had fallen off. I'm not sure why the sight of a shoe lying on its side a few inches from her foot was the thing that nearly made me cry. I turned my eyes away.

Darren looked us over, Clover tucked under his arm. She didn't like being held with her legs dangling and began to squirm.

"Hold still," he commanded, not taking his eyes from the three of us. She grew still, looking back and forth from his face to mine, panting.

Baby girl, be still, that's a good girl. I did my best to beam my thoughts to her.

Below the cliff, the river rushed endlessly over rocks to make its white noise. Behind us, the sun was sinking down over the rim of the next hill, knitting the shadows of the tall, tall trees into the beginning of night. From high overhead I heard the "Scree! Scree!" cry of a hunting hawk. A memory of being at Girl Scout camp with my sister flashed on the backs of my eyes—nine years old, sitting on the ground side by side in a clearing among the loblolly pines, hearing the cry of a red tail hawk as we waited for the camp fire to be lit so we could sing rounds and listen to ghost stories.

Everything was gone.

All I had were ghost stories.

Soon, one of the ghost stories would be mine.

"Put her down. Please."

"The plans."

"You know I would give them to you if I could. They're gone. You blew them up."

"Recreate them."

"*I can't.*"

I raised my eyes and looked him in the face. He stared back. And finally believed that what I had said was true. I saw his shoulders go down a fraction of an inch in defeat. He shifted his weight as he began to turn Clover toward the chasm.

On the other side of Janie, I felt more than saw Andy move, trying to get to his feet to save her.

"Put the dog down, Darren."

I had no idea who had spoken. The woman's voice was familiar, but it wasn't Janie's. Darren froze, then slowly turned away from the river. He stared in our direction. It took a moment to realize he was looking over our heads at something—someone—beyond us.

"Put. Her. Down."

Lisa.

She stood just inside the clearing, looking exactly as she had the last time I'd seen her at the dog park. The same jeans, colorful plaid shirt tucked neatly into the waistband, white trainers with grass streaks on her feet. Cheeks pink from the climb up the trail.

And with anger. It wasn't visible at first, but it was there.

The gun in her hand was a new touch. It looked exactly like Darren's.

"Put her down, Darren. Now." Her eyes never left his face as she began to walk toward him with slow, measured steps. A ballroom dancer hearing the first notes of a tango and being drawn inexorably to her partner. Her gun was steady.

One step. Two. Three.

Just as slowly, he leaned forward and set Clover gently on the ground, his eyes never leaving Lisa. In a flash, Clover was in my lap, her head tucked into my arm, her whole body trembling. My hands, still tied behind my back, throbbed with the need to wrap my arms around her. All I could do was lean over her to keep her safe.

The dance in front of us continued, Darren waiting, Lisa moving one foot in front of the other. His fixed gaze was that of a cobra confronted by the snake charmer. Her gun was fixed unwaveringly on his chest. His gun trembled in his hand.

When she spoke I heard a slow, slow crescendo in the music of her voice.

"I never said anything, Darren. Never, in all these years. At first I didn't believe it, didn't want to believe it, and then I was too hurt. You never knew, did you? Never even noticed. Never cared. All those women. All those crooked deals. And when I finally knew you for the amoral, selfish bastard that you are—well, by then I just didn't care anymore." She gave a scornful little laugh. "And you didn't notice that either."

Two more steps.

"But I would never have believed that even you—" she paused as she closed the gap between them— "that even you, Darren—" one more step, and she halted in front of him. Her voice grated like coarse sand. "I never thought that even a slimy piece of filth like you would threaten to kill a dog."

The last light of the setting sun flared on their faces as they stared deep into each other's eyes. And then Lisa reached out suddenly with the hand not holding her gun shoved him in the middle of the chest. He had been so focused on her gun that he didn't see it coming. His hand flew up, his gun went off, and he went backward over the cliff.

When his scream had faded into the white noise of the river, Lisa turned to survey my companions and me. She blinked once.

"There are some things," she said calmly, "that a wife simply cannot put up with."

27

AFTER

Two days passed before Darren's body, snagged by a tree that had fallen part way across the river, was found by three fourteen-year-old boys who had skipped school to go fishing. Lisa had reported him missing after twenty-four hours; the woman police officer who came to her house in response to her call was sympathetic, but cautious.

"You know, ma'am, there's really nothing we can do at this point. When an adult with no history of mental impairment goes missing, it's usually voluntary."

Lisa had nodded, dry eyed. "I—I just thought I should report it. He's never done anything like this before."

If there had been a slight emphasis on the word 'this' the officer seemed not to notice.

When his body was found, the autopsy showed he had drowned. A blow to the head had happened before and more battering after he died, but the coroner declared that everything was consistent with an accidental death. He had fallen in the river in an unknown spot, hitting his head, and was probably unconscious when he went under. Very sad. A loss to the community. Lisa had the body cremated, as her husband had wished, and on Saturday a well-attended memorial service was held.

Janie, Andy and I did not attend.

The following day was a sunny, crisp Sunday. The kind of day everyone wants to spend outdoors. Across Salem, lawns were mowed, late season tomatoes were plucked from back yard vines, and Bush's Pasture Park was full of walkers and picnickers. We took Clover, Tuffy and Piper to the dog park and watched them glory in the moment. And a young couple from Dearborn, Michigan, visiting the Pacific Northwest on their first vacation since their honeymoon two years earlier, found a trail that looked like a nice hike. Another vehicle was parked at the trail head. The path led up the side of a hill, not too steep, and eventually ended in a clearing surrounded by tall Douglas firs. The rushing sound of a river could be heard below a precipice on the left.

The body of a middle-aged woman lay unmoving in the dancing shadows, one shoe tumbled on the ground beside her. The sight of the gunshot wound sent the young couple back down the path much more quickly than they had come up.

The car parked at the trail head was quickly identified as Darren's SUV. The woman's body had no identification on it, but her fingerprints matched those on the passenger side of the SUV. They also matched those of a twice-convicted felon named Carlie Wilkinson, who had served time for forgery and credit card fraud. She had a long list of aliases on record. None of them were remotely close to Beth Harding.

When the identification came in, the officer who had taken Lisa's missing person report on Darren returned to see her, accompanied by a detective. She told them truthfully that she didn't know anyone named Carlie Wilkinson, but reluctantly admitted that her husband sometimes had affairs. The officers were sympathetic, and warned her to prepare herself for an onslaught of publicity.

"The bullet that killed her was from the same kind of gun that was registered to your husband," Detective Quint told her. "It's pretty clear that they went up there together, then most likely got into an argument. We'll never know if he shot her on purpose or if it was an accident, or whether he jumped into the river or somehow fell. It's quite a high drop at that spot."

Lisa listened mutely, stroking Chester's furry head.

"Was your husband in any kind of trouble? Any money problems?"

"No, at least not that I knew of. But—well, our marriage was...rocky. I was considering contacting a lawyer for a divorce."

"Did he know you planned to divorce him?"

"I don't think so. He didn't pay much attention to me anymore."

When the officers left, Lisa called Janie. "Hi, it's Lisa. Can you guys meet me and Chester at the dog park? Half an hour? Great, see you there."

Later that day, when we left the dog park to return to the apartment over the thrift store, Janie called her old friend Valerie Frost. "Valerie? Janie. We need to talk. Bring Martin Linder with you."

The four of us sat around Janie's dining table, an untouched cup of coffee steaming in front of each of us.

Linder seemed incapable of speech. Valerie kept repeating, "Oh, my god. Oh my god."

Janie let the news she had given them sink in, then said, "We may be able to skate through this."

"How? As soon as her picture comes out in the paper, all the staff are going to know it was her. Working at Willamette Environmental under someone else's name." Valerie closed her eyes as if in pain. "We'll be a laughingstock."

"I don't think so. Not if we get our story straight," I told her.

She opened her eyes. "Are you...were you really Mary Claire?"

I wasn't wearing Mary Claire's wig or glasses, but I cast my eyes down shyly and said in Mary Claire's Boston voice, "Yes ma'am, I surely was."

Linder spoke at last. "But you really *are* Dr. Beth Harding?"

"Yes, I am. I don't have much on me to produce by way of identification, but I suggest you send both my picture and one of Carlie Wilkinson to my attorney in North Carolina. She will be able to verify which of us is real. If you need more, I can give you the address and phone of my first grade teacher, Mrs. Eleanora Ewing. She's known me since I was five. Actually, you should probably use Skype to contact her. She loves to Skype, and even though she's ninety-three I can assure you she is still cherishing all her marbles."

He nodded. "We will do that, but I'm confident you'll check out. Your voice sounds familiar from our phone interviews."

"As does yours. Tell me, did your daughter get into MIT?"

He lit up. "You remember that! Yes, she did."

"While it's all well and good that you are really Beth Harding, what is going to happen when staff sees that other woman's picture in the paper?" Valerie said.

"They may not recognize her," Janie replied.

I nodded. "It depends on what picture they use. In college she wore her hair quite differently. I doubt she kept the same appearance for very long at a time. After all, she's been in prison twice."

"They could even run something like a mug shot," Janie said, "and if they do no one is going to connect her with the woman who worked at WETCo for such a short time."

"Plus I'm pretty sure the police have not connected her with my name," I added.

"It was so lucky she didn't have that driver's license she showed me with her," Valerie said.

Janie and I exchanged glances.

"Darren didn't give any of us a chance to grab our purses before he kidnapped us," I pointed out. "But with her fingerprints on file, there was no need for the police to look for ID."

"If anyone *does* remark on a resemblance," Janie said, "just look at the picture and say hmmm, maybe, but I really can't see it."

"But how do we explain her disappearance?"

"I'm sure you would never discuss a personnel matter," I said, "but somehow the scuttlebutt could get around that she was found dead drunk in her office at ten o'clock in the morning and you had no choice but to fire her. You won't have to say anything. Andy could plant a tidbit or two of gossip and the grapevine will take over."

Relief washed over Valerie's face, and a tiny smile played on her lips. "It's so odd how these things get about."

A frown furrowed the CEO's brow. "But Dr. Harding, what about you? What about the rain project?"

"There is no rain project." I made my voice as flat as possible. "If there is anyone you need to tell, you can say we hoped there was something to the idea, but it turned out to be unworkable."

"My telling Darren certainly turned out to be a mistake." Linder's voice held grief. "We were friends for years, and I had no idea who he really was."

"I just hope he was holding it close to the vest until he had the goods."

Valerie looked alarmed. "You mean—could there be others coming after your device?"

I sighed. "I have no way to know. If he had a buyer lined up who thought the work was complete, it's possible. I know I may never be truly safe." I paused to look Martin Linder in the eyes. "We have to end the project now."

"But it could be so important," Linder said. "We could keep it secret, I'm sure we could. Think what your device could mean."

"I've thought of little else since we first conceived of the project." I bit my lip, remembering talking late into the night with my twin, considering the ramifications of being able to make rain.

"The eventual depletion of the world's oil supplies will be as nothing compared to the water shortages I fear are in our children's future." The CEO's voice was pleading.

"I'm sorry." I bit my lip and willed the sting of tears away from my eyes. "I'm truly sorry. But it's over. Gone. I can't. I'm so sorry I got you and your company involved. If anyone needs to know anything, say it was a dream. Just a crazy dream."

For now, I've decided to stay in Salem. Clover and I still sleep in Jasper's loft bed, though when he came home for Thanksgiving we gladly relinquished his room to him and slept on Janie's couch. Before he went back to Vermont he gave me a couple of lessons in wall climbing. I hope to be able to make it all the way to the top before he's here for spring break. Clover runs up the spiral stairs and hangs over the edge, ready to give me doggy kisses the first time I make it up that high.

I've been helping in the thrift store and have gotten very good at making used clothing look nearly new. Andy works with us part time; he left Willamette Environmental when the income from his blog grew enough to pay the bills. We are the only ones (besides his brewing bartender friend) who know that he is the famous Betsy behind the Bitsy Betsy style blog.

Sometimes we see Lisa and Chester at the dog park. We smile and wave and give Chester a treat as they pass by.

This being Oregon, the rainy season has returned. Many days are gray and wet, but sunny ones return every week or so. We never speak of the sight of a column of rain falling on a golden hillside under its own personal rainbow.

Just lately I've started having a dream about Johnny Appleseed. I'm sure the real John Chapman bore little resemblance to the legend, but it's the legend I've had on my mind. Something about the idea of traveling around, doing good for people, and moving on catches at me.

Hell, maybe it's the Lone Ranger I'm thinking of.

But I have plenty of time, and plenty of money. I have a small device, its pieces still wrapped up in Janie's back pack. Clover carries three tiny silver disks inside her collar. And when I told Darren I didn't have the plans in my head, I lied.

I know exactly how it was made, and how it could be made bigger.

Is the human race ready to be able to produce rain at will? I don't know which I fear more, the ecological implications, or the dominance it would give to the power-mad if it were controlled by the wrong hands.

I think about all this, and about my sister and what she would have wanted me to do.

Sometimes I see Janie and Andy looking at me speculatively, wondering.

Am I Beth or Georgette?

Sometimes even I'm not sure.

THE END

ABOUT THE AUTHOR

Sharon Henegar started life in the Midwest, and although she is *not* in the Witness Protection Program she has lived in 27 houses in seven states. She now resides in a Midcentury Modern house in Salem, Oregon with her storyteller husband, Steven; Zoe, the Springer spaniel-mix dog who looks suspiciously like Clover; and Mrs. Wilberforce, an elderly cat. Together they conduct retreats for writers and storytellers.

She is the author of the Willow Falls mystery series, including *Sleeping Dogs Lie, In Dogs We Trust,* and *The Dog Prince.* Her blog, *Queen of Fifty Cents,* chronicles her adventures in thrifting. Her latest book is *Shopping on Driveways: Advice for Thrifters from the Queen of Fifty Cents.*

Henegar believes in home cooking, the restorative powers of humor and dogs, in buying secondhand, that a convertible should be driven with the top down, that life needs dessert, and that M&Ms should be bought in bulk. She is currently working on the next book in her Willow Falls series.

www.ingramcontent.com/pod-product-compliance
Lightning Source LLC
Chambersburg PA
CBHW060549260626
47161CB00003B/1116